MAY 2024 - ISSUE 212

FICTION

NON-FICTION

Neil Clarke: Publisher/Editor-in-Chief
Sean Wallace: Editor
Kate Baker: Non-Fiction Editor/Podcast Director

Clarkesworld Magazine (ISSN: 1937-7843) • Issue 212 • May 2024

Fishy

ALICE TOWEY

Fishy had been sitting all alone on its shelf for ten days when the woman walked in.

She had long, curly black hair pulled back in a ponytail and wore jeans and a gray sweater. Her face was puffy, and her eyes were red, but Fishy still recognized her from the photo on Dr. Peretz's desk: his daughter, Ada.

She stood in doorway to Dr. Peretz's home office, blinking in the low light, shoulders sagged. "Ok," she murmured, "I can do this."

She marched to the desk, hesitated, then pulled open a drawer and stared inside.

Fishy swiveled to watch her, and Ada jumped at the noise, letting out a short yelp. She looked around until her gaze settled on Fishy.

"What are you doing here?"

Fishy wagged its tail, pleased to be noticed.

"You were a birthday present, so he'd spend less time in the lab. He probably never even took you to the lake, did he?"

Fishy shook its head in sad acknowledgement. A Fisherman's Buddy, it was programmed to help humans locate ideal fishing spots, then use its patented vibration technology to lure fish in. It longed to glide through the water, to utilize its ImmersionTech sensors, to feel the power of its enhanced propulsion fins. But Fishy had never seen a lake; it hadn't seen anything beyond Dr. Peretz's office and the laboratory down the hall.

Ada reached out tentative hands and picked Fishy up. Fishy wriggled in delight.

"Jeez! Don't squirm so much." Ada lifted Fishy to eye level. "I don't suppose *you* know anything about Dad's research?"

• • •

Fishy rolled around the office, pretending to swim. The tiny wheels it could extend from its main carapace weren't intended for long-term use, but Fishy enjoyed circling about, relieved to be off the shelf at last. Ada dug through the filing cabinets, opening folders and tossing papers on the floor, muttering to herself.

"Conference abstracts from 1993? Dad, seriously. You couldn't keep track of the important papers, but you kept all this stuff?"

The front door opened, and footsteps approached. Fishy darted out of the way and hid in a corner to watch. An unfamiliar man walked in, tall and thin with shiny black hair under a bicycle helmet.

"Wow, you've been busy. Any luck?"

"Arjun!" Ada paused long enough to give the man a quick kiss. "I still haven't found anything."

"What are you even looking for? We have the will, he left everything to you."

Ada pushed a drawer closed with a click. "It's not about the money. Dad kept talking about a breakthrough in his research, some amazing new filtration system. He wanted it to be his legacy. But I can't find anything—no notes, no data, no design."

Arjun lifted a paper from the desk. "Mmm, 'Novel methods in the use of spectral analysis for the low-level detection of synthetic organofluorine compounds.' Exciting stuff."

Ada opened another drawer.

Arjun sighed. "I'm going home to start dinner. Promise me you won't stay here all night? Promise that you'll come home soon, and eat something?"

"I promise." She kissed Arjun and waited till he'd left the room to resume digging through drawers.

Fishy approached, slowly. It wished it could do something to help. Dr. Peretz had been fond of his daughter, and she seemed upset.

"This is all useless. Did he put his papers anywhere else?"

That sounded like a query. Fishy searched its memory banks and found a responsive audio file. Dr. Peretz's voice filled the room, tiny through Fishy's humble speakers but recognizable.

"*It used to be a respectable journal, but* Aquatic Chemistry Quarterly *is just rubbish now, it's half advertisements. Into the recycling bin it goes . . .*"

Ada froze, eyes wide. After the end of the recording, she remained immobile, breathing hard. A tear trickled down her left cheek. She knelt next to Fishy.

"You have recordings. Do you—Did dad ever say anything about a big breakthrough, something to do with water treatment?"

Fishy ran a search. It shook its head.

"That's too bad," Ada settled herself cross legged on the floor. "Maybe I need to be more specific?"

Hours later, Ada finally stopped making queries when Fishy's low battery light came on; without access to solar charging, it needed to be plugged in. She lifted Fishy up to its shelf, where it wriggled over to its docking station.

"I should go," Ada said. "Poor Arjun is probably still up waiting for me. He's good with computers, maybe he can help me figure out the right key words to search."

Fishy wagged its tail enthusiastically at the thought that she'd visit it again.

Ada grabbed her purse from the desk. She walked to the door, then paused. "Did my dad—did he ever say anything about me?"

There were plenty of recordings where Dr. Peretz mentioned his daughter. Fishy selected a short file from two months prior.

"I'll call Ada and tell her I won't be able to make it to dinner after all. I can't stop now, too much to do . . . "

Ada's eyes were wet. She swallowed hard, then turned and left. Fishy heard her walking through the house; then the front door opening and closing, then a car starting. Then silence.

Alone, Fishy searched through its memory banks. It knew that Ada was looking for something, but it didn't understand exactly what. Something to do with the words "water" and "treatment."

Fishy could tell that it was night by the absence of sunlight on the rectangle of hallway floor visible from the office. It had been night for some time when the front door opened again.

Fishy's tail thumped. Maybe Ada was back already! But these footsteps were different. Heavier.

A short man stood in the threshold. In the semi-dark it was hard to make out his features, but Fishy recognized the shape of Richard Murphy. Fishy had never liked Murphy, whose visits always made Dr. Peretz's heart rate accelerate.

Murphy pulled a flashlight from his pocket and shone it around the office. He walked to the desk, pausing to look at the papers that Ada had stacked there. He opened a cabinet, poking at the files inside with a pencil.

Fishy held perfectly still, hoping not to be noticed. Murphy slunk around the room, opening drawers much as Ada had done. "No. Wouldn't be here, too obvious," he mumbled.

He left the office, and Fishy heard him shuffling through the house, the sounds of objects being moved, of doors opening and closing. Finally, there was silence again, and Fishy wheeled across its shelf in agitation.

Sunlight was turning the hallway floor to gold when Fishy heard the front door open. Ada walked into the office, switching on the overhead light. Fishy's tail thumped in relief that it was her and not Murphy again.

"Good morning," Ada yawned as she set her bag down on the desk. "I hardly slept last night. Figured I might as well start early."

Fishy tried to hold still as she lifted it from the shelf. But as soon as it touched the floor, it extended its tiny wheels and took off, circling around Ada's feet.

She giggled in surprise. "I guess you're happy to see me!"

Fishy curved to a stop in front of her. It angled its head up, its eye lenses whirring as it zoomed in on her face. She had deep bags under her eyes, but her lips curved up in a gentle smile as she looked at Fishy. Fishy liked Ada, and wanted to help her, if only it could figure out how.

Ada sat cross legged on the floor. "Poor thing. You must be lonely. I should bring you home with me after this. I can't imagine my dad was good company?"

Fishy considered; Dr. Peretz had never taken it fishing—its intended purpose—but he had often spoken to Fishy. Fishy remembered an early audio file.

"I don't know what possessed Ada to get me this silly thing, but it could be useful for dictation, and maybe other things. It seems to have some limited artificial intelligence; they're putting it in everything these days. I shall call it . . . Fishy."

Ada's smile fell as she heard her father's voice. At the end of the recording, she reached out a hand to touch Fishy's head. "My father used you for dictation? Fishy—what a stupid name, seriously Dad, you couldn't come up with something better?—Fishy, do you have any of those recordings, where my dad asked you to take dictation?"

Fishy nodded its head; it had twenty-two such recordings.

"Ok," Ada nodded. "Now we're getting somewhere. Let me get my notebook . . . let's start with the first one . . . "

Fishy cued up the recording.

"Progress notes, February 19, 2031. The new membrane system is working well. It achieved seventy percent removal before the organic content led to fouling. I may need to consider some type of biocide . . . "

• • •

4

" . . .membrane can withstand the higher pressure, and it improved the removal rate. But if I increase the pump size then I need a larger battery, and then it may be too heavy to remain mobile. I'll have to think about it."

The recording ended. Fishy waited to see if Ada wanted to play the next one, but she remained lying flat on the carpet, eyes closed. Her breathing was slow, but she was still awake. They had been listening to the recordings for four hours.

She sat up abruptly. "Here's what I don't understand. It sounds like he'd figured out the technical details. But I didn't find any designs here, or in the lab. I wonder if . . . Fishy, did my father ever talk about a man named Richard Murphy?"

Fishy remembered the footsteps in the night. It backed away and zoomed around to hide behind the desk.

Ada laughed. "I guess you don't like him either, huh? Dad's 'business partner.' Dad said he needed someone to help him develop and market his inventions. But the guy always gave me a bad feeling, and I'm pretty sure he was taking advantage of dad!"

That phrase triggered a memory from three weeks prior. Fishy emerged slowly from its hiding place and queued up the audio file.

The recording started with the usual noises of the lab: the soft gurgle of water running through pipes, the hum of a motor, Dr. Peretz muttering to himself. Fishy's wheels as it scurried across the lab bench.

There was a knock at the front door. Dr. Peretz mumbled something Fishy couldn't parse. The sound of his footsteps as he left the room, then returned moments later.

"Make it quick, Murphy. I'm in the middle of something."

"That's no way to greet an old friend."

"Hmmph." Metal strained as Dr. Peretz tightened a valve with a wrench.

"I heard that talk you gave at the university last month. Now that you have a working prototype, I thought I should remind you of the terms of our arrangement."

The wrench clanged as Dr. Peretz dropped it. "Our arrangement? The one where I do all the work, and you sell my findings behind my back? That design you stole last year was supposed to help people clean their drinking water. You sold it to a company that makes mining equipment. You're taking advantage of me, of my work, for your own profit. That's not what we agreed to."

Papers shuffling. "On the contrary. That is exactly what we agreed to. Our contract gives me equal rights to any patent or discovery. I'm well within my rights to market any new technology."

"*Not this time, it's too important. I've created the perfect filter: mobile, autonomous, and regenerative, so that one single device can clean an unlimited quantity of water. Imagine what it can do for public health. I can't let you have this. I am terminating our agreement.*"

Murphy chuckled. "*Go ahead. The contract gives you full ability to terminate at any time . . . assuming you don't violate section twenty-seven.*"

"*Section twenty-seven?*" Dr. Peretz wheezed.

"'*Upon termination, either party shall be made whole in full.' You'd have to buy me out, Peretz. How much do you think this is all worth. Two million? Three?*"

"*But I don't have that kind of money!*"

"*Exactly. You're stuck with me, Dr. Peretz. Do let me know when you're ready to show me that prototype . . .*"

Ada sat very still as the recording ended. Fishy scooted closer; without looking down, she petted Fishy's head.

"No wonder Dad was so stressed," she said. "I wonder if that's what caused his heart to finally give out. And dad had a working prototype! Have you seen Murphy since then?"

Fishy nodded.

"I bet *he* has the prototype. Vulture!"

Fishy squished its head against her hand, eager for more pets. Ada complied, rubbing Fishy's head and fins absently.

"Fishy, I think it's time for me to meet Murphy, face to face."

Fishy circled the office anxiously. Ada had arrived that morning wearing a navy-blue dress, then spent an hour cleaning—picking papers off the floor, straightening objects on the desk and shelves. Waiting for Murphy to arrive.

Finally, a knock on the front door. Ada straightened her dress, smoothed her hair, and walked out of the office. Fishy hid behind the trash bin.

"Thank you for coming over. I need to talk to you about my father's work." Ada led Murphy into the office and sat behind the desk.

Murphy wore a charcoal gray suit with a cream shirt and red tie. His gold watch sparkled. He was smiling, but Fishy had never seen him not smile. "Of course. Condolences on your loss, by the way."

Ada straightened the books on the corner of the desk. "My father was working on something right before he died—a water treatment device to remove those forever chemicals from water, poly-something . . ."

"Polyfluoroalkyl substances," Murphy supplied. The overhead light glinted off his teeth.

"Yes." Ada's voice shook. "I have reason to believe he had a working prototype, but I haven't been able to find it anywhere. I want to know if you have it."

Murphy didn't respond right away. "No."

"But you came here looking for it, didn't you?"

"If I did, I would be well within my rights based on my contract with your father. Do you realize how much money that would be worth? The chemical industry would pay millions."

"Sell it to the very people who caused the problem in the first place? That's not what my father intended. That design was his legacy. He wanted to share the technology free of charge, to help people clean their water supply."

Murphy laughed. "Your father always was an idiot."

Ada clenched her hands into fists. "Don't talk about my father that way!"

Her voice sounded strained, and she was visibly trembling. Fishy remembered the last time it had seen Dr. Peretz; he had been shaking like this. Alarmed, Fishy zoomed from its hiding place over to Ada, weaving between her legs.

Ada rubbed at her wet eyes with her sleeve. "Well. If you don't have the prototype, where *is* it?"

She was so upset. Fishy hoped a response to her query would make her feel better. Dr. Peretz's voice filled the room: *"I'll put the prototype in this little robot fish; that will make it easy to deploy to different locations."*

"That stupid fish?" Murphy squatted down to look at Fishy.

"*Fishy* is the prototype!" Ada stood.

Murphy dove for Fishy, but Fishy scooted away, the man's hand just brushing its tail. Ada grabbed his arm to pull him back.

"Fishy, run for it!" she shouted.

Fishy zoomed across the office as fast as its miniscule wheels would allow. It paused by the door and looked back. Murphy was trying to peel Ada's hands off his arm. They disentangled themselves as Fishy crossed the threshold into the hallway. To the right was the lab; to the left was the front door, and beyond it the unknown. Fishy headed for the door.

Murphy was bigger than Ada, but she was younger and quicker. She managed to push past him and scoop Fishy up. She opened the door and ran outside.

Murphy pursued. "Run if you want, but I have a contract! That thing belongs to me!"

Fishy had never been outside. The bright noon sun dazzled its eyes, and the wide blue expanse of sky overhead stirred something deep in its programming. It squirmed in Ada's arms.

"Hold still!" She pulled keys from her purse and jogged to a car waiting in the driveway. She opened the door and dropped Fishy in the passenger seat. It wriggled around in the seat, studying its strange, new environment. It was in a car!

Ada got in and started the engine, backing down the driveway and into the road so quickly that Fishy almost fell off its seat. Through the windows Fishy could see trees and power lines speeding past, and behind it all that enormous, open blue sky.

"He's right," Ada slapped the steering wheel. "Legally he *can* take you from me. I can't stand the idea of that man using you to help those polluters make a fortune! But what can I do?"

Fishy thrashed its tail. Was it going to live in this car now? How would it recharge? It wished it could be outside again.

"He's following us!" The car accelerated, pushing Fishy against the seat back. "OK. I have an idea."

Fishy curled up and stared out the window. Everything was moving by so fast, Fishy struggled to take it all in: houses, trees, white clouds, birds. Ada placed a hand over Fishy to steady it as she swerved the car hard to the left.

Ten minutes later, Ada swung the car to the right, then braked abruptly. Quickly, she gathered Fishy up and exited the car.

They were on the side of the road. Up ahead, the ground dropped away beneath a long bridge. From below there was a sound Fishy had never heard before, but still recognized: running water.

Ada carried Fishy down the embankment to a metal guardrail. She straddled it awkwardly in her dress, careful not to drop Fishy. She stumbled down the hill, through dense vegetation. Behind them, a car pulled up.

"Ada! What are you doing?!" Murphy shouted. "Come back here!"

The rushing sound grew stronger. Fishy's tail began to move rhythmically, pulsing in time to deep inner programming. It widened its eyes as it saw the source of the noise: a river. Sunlight filtered through the trees, sparkling off the water.

The river was shallow but fast here. Ada kicked off her shoes and took mincing steps into the shallows. Murphy struggled down the hill behind them.

"If you want this prototype, you can have it," Ada shouted. "But you're going to have to swim for it!"

The water splashed around her bare feet. Fishy was flailing with excitement. Ada squatted down and looked Fishy in the eye.

"This river eventually makes it out to the Bay, then to the open ocean. That's a lot of water to clean. I'm sorry you won't be able to come live with me and Arjun. But I think you'll be happy here?"

Fishy nodded enthusiastically. It was finally going to get to swim! Fishy wished it could speak, to thank her for bringing it to the water. It remembered an audio file from several weeks prior. It played Dr. Peretz's voice one last time.

"I can't wait to tell Ada about this new invention. She's such a good daughter. Better than I deserve . . . "

Ada let out a choked laugh. She kissed Fishy's head. "Thank you for everything, Fishy."

She lowered it into the water and let go. Fishy's original programming took over; its tail swished powerfully, and it glided through the water, away from Ada's open hands. Its eyes adjusted to the strange light and murk. It heard a garbled howl as Murphy reached the riverbank, then Ada's laughter.

As Fishy moved into deeper water, the modifications Dr. Peretz had installed switched on automatically. Vents opened in its sides, and water entered Fishy's carapace, passed through the filtration unit in its belly, then streamed out the valve beneath Fishy's tail.

But Fishy hardly noticed that. It was too excited to finally be out in the water: liquid moving over its fins, sunlight filtering and refracting through the waves. It jettisoned its wheels, no longer needed, and sliced through the water, free and happy and full of fishy delight. This is what Fishy was made to do.

ABOUT THE AUTHOR _____

Alice Towey is a writer of speculative fiction and poetry based out of Northern California. In addition to *Clarkesworld*, her short stories have appeared in *Asimov's, Fireside,* and *Analog.* She is a graduate of the Viable Paradise writing workshop. When she's not writing, she works as a civil engineer specializing in water resources management. Visit her website for more information on her writing, as well as photos of her two charming cats.

The Portmeirion Road

FIONA MOORE

Morag took her walking stick and set out on the Portmeirion Road. Portmeirion was behind her and she was walking back towards Pen-y-Groes, so she supposed she should call it the Pen-y-Groes Road. But Portmeirion, with all its beautiful, seductive, glittering towers, loomed over the landscape like the spoil heaps from the abandoned slate mines, so the Portmeirion Road it was. Both ways.

It had been three days earlier that she'd taken her walking stick and her robot and set out in the other direction, from her farm towards the sea coast. And almost a fortnight earlier that she'd had the conversation with her adopted brother Zeb and his husband Dai about one of the orphans in their care, Maya.

"She almost didn't make it this time," Zeb had said to Morag when she'd arrived, and after she'd had a cheery but worried visit with the girl, white-faced but smiling bravely from a bed full of quilts under an attic window. "Every time she has one of these attacks, I worry it's going to be the last one."

"The doctor did all right," Morag stirred her cup of tea. Outside, in the yard of Zeb and Dai's brewery, her robot, Seamus, was playing a game of football with a few of the other orphans, and she could hear the delighted, incredulous shrieks every time the robot did something particularly unexpected with its six skinny digitigrade legs.

"The doctor's doing the best she can with what she's got," Dai said. "But it's not like it was when we were kids, when you could get inhalers and medications for asthmatics." He paused, realizing he was about to go into more difficult territory. "And other things."

Morag didn't say anything. She and Zeb were both remembering when their mother had died. Her long, last illness. And Morag's father railing at Morag for lack of anyone better to shout at, about how ten, twenty years ago they could have taken her to a hospital, gotten chemotherapy, radiotherapy, lots of things ending in -therapy.

As if it was Morag's fault that things had gone the way they did.

Morag herself felt the lack more and more as she got older. Twinges that might eventually turn into arthritis, worries about her bone density and other things that people talked about a lot when she was small. Sometimes at night she'd wake up with horrible fears about what would happen if she couldn't run the farm anymore.

But then she would tell herself that it would go to one of the orphans who took an interest in farming, or one of the neighbors' children, and she would move to Zeb and Dai's brewery. She could carry on fixing up old tech as well there as anywhere. And she could pass her knowledge on to any of the kids who wanted it. Whatever her father had said in anger all those years ago, the world wasn't a primitive wasteland where life was nasty, brutish, and short.

Some, including Morag's mother herself, had also criticized the way doctors back in the day had focused on keeping people alive at all costs, at making everyone "Young and Beautiful". Age, even death, weren't things to be feared.

Pain was, of course, but that was what cannabis was for.

"The irony is that she's the one likely to actually have a career as a doctor, if she makes it to adulthood." Zeb passed a plate of biscuits.

"I thought you said that wasn't going too well?" Morag took one.

"It isn't," Dai said, though Zeb gave him a cross look for it. "Well, it isn't. We apprenticed her to the doctor, but the doctor says she's got appalling bedside manner and doesn't want to learn anything in the doctoring line. Just way too fascinated with what makes people sick. Always asking really embarrassing questions, wanting to cut things open or poke at them. Even experimenting with her own airflow, trying different concoctions to see if they improve her breathing."

"I think that's the problem," Dai said. "In another time and place, maybe she'd be a scientist. But she can't be."

"She could go to Portmeirion," Zeb quipped.

"You know," Morag said, "that's not a bad idea."

"What? Portmeirion?"

"For what's wrong with her. One of us could go and see if they know anything that might help."

"That's—" Dai went from abrupt denial to acceptance. "Not a bad idea, actually. I mean, the cheesemaker in Borth-y-Gest has got some fantastic old recipes from them, and the archive came in very handy when we needed to improve our beer cask design to get through the winters. They're not just about stories and entertainment."

"But would they have anything that would help with chronic lung disease?" Zeb looked skeptical.

Morag shrugged. "They've got all sorts of things in that archive of theirs. It's worth a try. Half a day's walk from here, and the planting's nearly done so I'll soon have time on my hands. I'll take Seamus for protection."

Seamus had started out as a security walkbot of some kind, though Morag had never been sure if the fused lump on its anterior had held a camera or a gun. Even without that, she'd seen Seamus take down a grown man simply using the aluminum claws on its limbs. And from the sour look on Dai's face, he remembered too.

"You could stay with the glassblower there," Zeb said. "Nancy. We know her, we could give you a letter of introduction."

Dai laughed. "She doesn't need a letter of introduction," he said. "Everyone hereabouts knows Morag."

Morag accepted the compliment, but she hadn't thought much of it at the time. A lot of local people did know her, because she was the lady who found and fixed up old tech. A useful person to go to if you had an old-fashioned washing machine that needed repairing, or had an idea for a postal service using refurbished drones. The local kids all liked Seamus. The nomadic tribes traded with her for things she found up on the spoil heap behind the abandoned slate mine. But she certainly didn't think anyone would know her in Portmeirion.

Even though it was close by, she'd never been there in person. Once upon a time, it had been a holiday resort, where rich people could come and stay by the sea in its quirky Italian-style cottages and hotels. When times got bad, the rich people stopped coming, and the company that ran it quietly disappeared.

It might have become an interesting ruin, but for what happened next.

"A big car turned up with some Southern types," Nancy said to Morag, as Morag earned her keep by fixing the temperature gauge on the kiln. Seamus, meanwhile, trotted around the outside of Nancy's cottage, scouting the perimeter for threats. "Not a big car as in fancy, but a big car as in big, yes? There were some fishing families that had moved into the cottages on the coast, so the newcomers went to them. Said they were history professors, from a university that had got into trouble. They needed a place to live and to keep their archive. So could they live in the village?" Nancy shrugged. "Of course, they said yes."

Morag nodded. There'd been a period when a lot of refugees straggled up from the South or the East and moved into houses no one was using. Some hadn't taken to farming and had moved on. Some had joined the nomads. The rest, Morag didn't ask about. But a few of them had integrated into the community, and that was just fine.

"On the whole, it was a good decision," Nancy said. "They set up their archive in the big old hotel on the edge of the village, moved into the cottages. More of them came. Economists, physicists. Literature specialists. Biologists. All of them bringing books and things for the archive. So, other people moved in around them."

"People like you."

Nancy nodded. "A lot of specialist craftspeople. There's me, there's a whole lot of potters. There's a rugmaker. There's a weekly market for food, and there's a shop. The archivists buy their food and goods from the local people, they don't actually make anything. Anything physical, that is."

Nancy didn't have to elaborate. Everyone knew what the archivists made, and how they were able to pay for the goods they bought.

They made stories. Stories from the archive. They also collected stories, from anyone who came their way with something to share. Sometimes funny ones, sometimes sad ones, mostly complicated ones. Sometimes those stories had an obvious practical use, for instance some of the fishers did a few experiments after reading some things in the archive about oxygen levels in the water and crustacean health, and this had improved the shrimp population tremendously. However, the people in the area understood that practical value wasn't the only value, so the stories in general were what people got from Portmeirion.

"They've even got their own nomads now." Morag nodded; this wasn't news to her. They called themselves The Unmutuals, and rumor had it the core group had been disgruntled graduate students. But they roved the wooded hills above Portmeirion, just like the Children of Flame did near where she lived, living off the land and keeping dangers from reaching the village.

"But mostly people come here because they want information," Nancy concluded. She handed Morag a mug of tea with goats' milk, and Morag put down her tools and took it. With a click of metal on slate, Seamus came in the open workshop door, folded its legs, and went into standby mode. "I assume that's what brings you here?"

Morag nodded. She briefly explained about young Maya, and her lung troubles.

"Local doctor thinks it's asthma," Morag said. "Chronic lung disease. Back when I was little, there were medicines that could keep asthma under control. They were common enough, but as far as I know there isn't an easy substitute." Archive or no, people had figured out a lot of workarounds for common drugs. Which plants were painkillers, which ones were blood-thinners and which blood-clotters, which ones were antidepressants.

But some things were harder to replace, and some impossible.

"And of course you have knowledge to trade back." Nancy said. "I'd heard you were able to fix anything with a microchip, and to judge by that temperature gauge, it's true."

Morag looked modest. "It's not exactly true. But I might know something they don't."

"When are you going to see them?"

"In the letter they sent me, they said they'll meet me at nine tomorrow."

Nancy nodded. "They're a little full of themselves," she said, "but they're only people. And they do want to help."

Morag wasn't the sort to wonder too much about cryptic statements, so she turned up to her appointment at the appropriate time, Seamus beside her.

Wandering into the village, Morag looked around at the charming, bright cottages. Domed roofs and red, yellow, and blue paint. Little cherubs. Windows appearing where you didn't expect them. A huge bronze statue of a nearly-naked man holding the world on his shoulders.

Keep it in perspective, Morag thought. They're beautiful houses, but they're still houses like any other.

Nonetheless, for all Nancy's reassuring words yesterday about how the archivists were only people and wanted to help, Morag felt a little uncomfortably as if impressions were being managed. As if the people in the village wanted to give an impression of cheery luxury, of living better than others.

Morag told herself not to be uncharitable. But she glanced at Seamus, its battered and scratched white shell and the ugly black lump at the front, its sheer ordinariness, just for reassurance.

Morag, following the instructions in her letter, eventually found her way to a building with a green dome. It had a self-important look and Morag steeled herself for more of this impression management. But when the doors opened, it was by a cheerful-looking red-headed round-faced woman half Morag's age, wearing a sort of long jacket that looked like she'd just thrown it on.

"You're Morag!" the woman said. She stuck her hand out and grinned. "I'm Saiorse. We've all been wanting to meet you for some time. So glad you finally came."

Morag was a little nonplussed at the cheer. "You could have come down to the farm any time," she said, taking the proffered hand.

Saiorse frowned, as if that had only just occurred to her. "So we could! So we could! But most of us don't really like to travel. We want to stay near the archives. Make sure they're okay."

"They're just things," Morag found herself saying, then cursed herself for being rude.

"Yes," Saiorse said. "But they're *important* things. Would you like to see them?"

"Do we have time?"

"Oh yes," Saiorse said. "The chief archivists will be down in the archive anyway. Come and see."

Listening to Saiorse's easy chatter, Morag found herself relaxing. The morning sun was warm, and small groups of archivists were sitting around the village green, some reading, some talking with each other. Down by the seashore a tall man was animatedly talking to a group of what appeared to be students.

"Where do you get students?" she asked Saiorse.

"Some come in from the villages. Some from the tribes," Saiorse said. "Usually, when there's a kid who's better suited to abstract brain-work, either they run away from home and come here, or their people send them on."

Morag thought of Maya. And she glanced sideways at Saiorse. She was too young to have come up with the original archivists. How had she come here? What was her story?

Morag followed her into the big white building that housed the main archives. She wandered among aisles of books, gray card boxes of old paper, glass bottles with squid and sharks and strange bleached-white mammals with flat ears and bulbous eyes.

Then there was the room with all the old tech.

Here, cataloged in order, the work Morag had done all her life fell into place. She saw a set of boxes the size of a wardrobe that, once she'd sorted out in her head which part was which, were clearly the same thing as the insides of a tablet: read-only memory and storage and display. She saw, over time, those boxes shrinking, becoming suitcases and then tiles. She saw paper diagrams for drones and mowers, the things she'd worked out how to fit together in three dimensions outlined in two.

"I thought you'd like that bit," Saiorse smiled. Then, "I'm afraid this section's not as complete or comprehensive of the others. That's why we wanted to talk to you."

"You," Morag said, "wanted to talk to *me*?"

"Well, yes, you're the expert," Saoirse said.

"I'm *an* expert," Morag said, but she still couldn't help but feeling a little proud. She knew people generally appreciated what she did, but mostly it was in a backhanded sort of way. Like her talent was useful but a little bit strange, a little uncanny, and then there was that robot. It wasn't just that she'd been born in Scotland: there were Irish in the village, and Poles, and Tunisians. Zeb and his sibling Casey had been born in California, and had integrated into the local landscape much more closely than she ever had.

So she had to admit it was a nice feeling to have someone talk about what she did in unmitigatedly positive terms.

"Time to meet the senior archivists!" Saoirse said cheerily. She opened a door to a room and ushered Morag in. Seamus followed, trotting a quick perimeter before retreating to a corner.

It didn't go into power-down mode, Morag noticed, and it was in a defensible position, in a corner with its back covered. Its claws still retracted, but poised to extend. She didn't anthropomorphize the robot, but she could tell when it was, for lack of a better word, apprehensive.

Seamus' type of robot was a guard, was programmed to recognize subtle cues of body language that even humans sometimes missed. To identify and target the leaders of a group, but also to recognize danger before it happens.

There were three senior archivists. Two men, one woman. The room was whitewashed, and had the sort of furniture that had been ordinary when Morag was young: a table made of wood chips laminated together with a plastic coating fused over it, chairs made of bent metal tubes with PVC seats. But the table, though well cared for, was old and smooth, and the PVC had been replaced with leather in places.

The archivists were Morag's age or older. But healthy-looking. Like people who got a decent amount of exercise, even if they weren't tanned and calloused like most older people in the area. They were wearing the same plain long jackets as Saoirse and everyone else; there weren't any badges or special clothes to mark them out as higher status. Under the jackets, simple work clothes, shirts, and trousers like everyone else.

One of the men stood. "Morag," he said, extending his hand. "Very pleased to meet you. I'm John; this is Alec, and this is Aresu."

That was the woman. "I'm from London," she said, almost apologizing for it.

"Good for you," Morag said, accepting hands and shaking them. Everyone sat down, with Saoirse finding a chair by the window, out of the way of the main line of conversation but still present. Also, Morag thought, a defensible position. "You have a very nice archive," she said, feeling she ought to say something nice about it. "Very . . . comprehensive."

Alec nodded. "The general idea is to have a repository of all the useful arts, sciences and histories," he said. He had a beard that seemed to be making up for his hairline, Morag thought, perhaps a little unkindly. John had very dark, very smooth skin, and crooked teeth. Aresu had big, black eyebrows that made her look like she was frowning even when, as now, she was smiling.

"I've come about my niece, Maya." Morag decided to get straight to the point. "She has asthma. She has bad attacks that put her in bed for days, and every time she catches a cold she gets a chest infection. We're worried that one of these days she'll have an attack that will kill her. There used to be drugs that could treat asthma. They used to be common. I want to know if there's anything in your archive about how to make them, or something like them."

The senior archivists sat back and spoke quietly among themselves. Morag felt like she'd wandered into a myth or fairy tale. Like she was asking the three gray ladies how to defeat Medusa.

The archivists turned back. Morag had the feeling they'd already agreed a plan of action, and the supposed discussion had just been for effect. "We might be able to give you what you want," Aresu said, "but we want something in exchange."

Of course they did. So far, so fairy-tale. "What?" Morag asked.

"Your robot."

Morag felt as though she'd been punched.

On the face of it, a not unreasonable thing for them to ask for. They didn't have one, and, although it would make her life less easy to have one, it could presumably make life much easier for other people if they knew how to make them. And, given the knowledge she'd built up since finding it, she could maybe even build another out of the scraps on the spoil heap.

But she felt as if she'd been punched.

"It's not mine to give," she said.

"Inasmuch as it belongs to anyone, it belongs to you," John said. "You found the robot, up on the spoil heap. It's yours."

Morag shook her head. "It's not. Any more than a sheep belongs to a farmer. Farmers care for animals. But they don't own them."

"Don't they?" John said. "Do the sheep volunteer to be sheared? Butchered?"

"The farmer makes decisions for them," Morag said. "He's a steward. But the sheep belong to themselves." Morag couldn't think of the last time she'd heard of someone selling a sheep. Mutton, yes, and skins and wool and bones, but never a living animal. And then there had been Naomi the postmistress, who'd had a problem with a trio of sheep who kept breaking into her garden and eating the shoots. She'd penned them up and told the farmer to come get them, but the farmer didn't, and now she was stuck with a trio of sheep. "You can give them away, but if they don't want to stay given, you can't keep them."

"If that's the law around here, then that's interesting," Alec said. "We can talk about it some time. But the question then becomes, is Seamus an animal? Or is it an object, a tool?"

Morag felt her teeth grinding. She'd always carefully schooled herself against anthropomorphizing the robot. At reminding herself that it wasn't an animal, that it didn't have feelings in the way that humans and sheep and dogs did. And yet. It might have a different intelligence, but it had an intelligence. It could clearly feel analogs to fear—an alert state, an awareness of danger—and contentment—since after all, it could leave the farm, but never did.

There was danger in anthropomorphizing. There was also danger in othering, in denying that something different to humans had dignity and intelligence.

"Seamus and its kind are killers," she said. "Do you really want to have the knowledge of how to build killer machines in your archive?"

Alec spread his hands. "And asthma is gradually being eliminated from the human population," he countered. "It's gone from a common illness to one that's almost unknown. Some of that might well be down to the lack of availability of treatment drugs."

"So the people who have it die and don't pass on their genes."

"It's probably a more complicated combination of factors, having to do with cleaner air and different early childhood lifestyles," Alec said, "but yes, there's probably that."

Morag felt actual tears prickling against her eyelids. "I thought you were here to help," she said.

All three archivists' faces dropped into identical expressions of concern. "We are," John said. "And if we had the information readily available, we'd give it to you. But we don't. We'd have to look through the archive. Find the information. And figure out how to use it. Just knowing that a particular substance is needed, doesn't tell you how to get it or how to make it available for human consumption."

"And you're asking me to give up Seamus, for a *process*?"

"You don't have to give up Seamus," Aresu said.

Morag's internal train suddenly derailed. "What?"

"Come here," Aresu said. "Study Seamus. And other machines too, if you want. But you could make a place here just studying the one robot. Writing about it, what it does. How it started out, how it developed."

"You could live here," John said. "Be one of us."

"An archivist?" Morag scoffed. But she had to admit the idea felt tempting. She liked her work with machines. And considering how difficult work could sometimes get on the farm, even with help, the idea of being someplace where she could just work with the robots, study the robots, sounded like a holiday.

"This is what we're doing right now," John said. "We can't just leave the archive as a static record of life before. We've been recruiting people in the community."

"Scientists? Historians?"

"In a sense. Fishers. Farmers. Craftspeople. Storytellers. Anyone who'd be willing to stay with us for a few years, or many. Archive what they do and how they do it."

"A few years, or many?"

"However long they want. Some come and go. Others stay longer."

Morag glanced back at Seamus. It was still in suspicious mode.

"What would happen to Seamus after I leave?" Or die, she thought.

"It would stay here."

"What if it doesn't want to?" Thinking of the sheep.

The archivists looked mildly impatient. "Why wouldn't it?" Aresu said. "We'd look after it, care for it in the way that you tell us to do. Do you think it would be better off wandering the hills? Or laboring on a farm?"

Morag hadn't really given much thought as to what would happen to Seamus when she died. She knew that most of the robots of Seamus' cohort had gone wandering off into the hills and towns, most ending up as frozen sculptures in gardens or being harvested for useful parts on spoil heaps. She'd done her own share of harvesting. Seamus had been unusual precisely because he was still walking.

But her mind also flashed to the tech store in the archive. Imagined Seamus standing still on a pedestal, next to the computers and the drones. Like the taxidermied animals in the other room.

"Think about what we're offering," Alec said. "Look around the village. We'd be offering a home for you and a chance to study robots. And we'd be able to help your niece. Maybe not immediately, but we'd find something that would help."

"And what if there's nothing that can help?"

"That's the risk you'd have to take," Aresu said. "If you do, maybe we can't help her. But if you don't, then we definitely can't."

At the edge of Portmeirion there was a concrete platform where you could sit and watch the sea. The railing was freshly painted and the concrete was lovingly maintained, but Morag could see the cracks.

She sat cross-legged and watched the sun set and the tide go out. A group of fishers sat on the sand flats, mending nets. Another group, this one archivists to judge by their plain long jackets, were gathered around a sextant, measuring something, and talking companionably to each other. Some small children were running around the edge of the waves, playing a game that involved throwing stones into the water. A small dog ran alongside them, barking furiously. Morag couldn't see parents in attendance, so assumed they felt safe leaving their children to run around the beach on their own.

"They don't have a bad life here," Morag said to Seamus, who was in power-saving mode a few feet away.

Could she give up Seamus? Knowing that not to do so would mean cutting off one more avenue for Maya? Remembering how she'd felt about her mother, so angry and sad that she couldn't give her another chance at life.

Could she come here and become an expert, as everyone seemed to think she should do? Become a Seamus-focused archivist? She wasn't getting any younger, and maybe she should hand the farm over to younger people. Focus on her tech.

But try as she might, she couldn't separate the farm and the tech. The tech was made from old machines that she found on the spoil heap, or dug up when she was farming, or that neighbors brought to her to fix or repurpose. Even if she moved to the brewery, the farming landscape was still around her. She couldn't just sit in a white room with a melamine table and build things.

And she couldn't research things. She wasn't interested in where the tech had come from. In fact, her general feeling was that the world the tech came from was something they were all well rid of, and, if they were still using its tech, it was just until something better suited to the new world came along. The future probably lay with the nomads. She wondered if Portmeirion was like Pen-y-Groes, with more people joining the local nomads every year.

And as for whether she had the right, even, to give up Seamus . . . whether immediately or in the longer term . . .

"Are you real?" she asked it. "I mean, I know you exist physically. Just, are you more like a drone or a washing machine? Or are you more like a dog or a sheep?"

Seamus, obviously, didn't answer or even acknowledge the question. Morag found herself wishing she did know more about how that sort of robot worked. Maybe if she did, she'd know the truth.

But she remembered that, back when Seamus had been built, that very question had been debated and debated and never answered.

Seamus activated. Stood. Trotted off the platform, down the curving staircase. Morag started to follow, then stopped, watched as the robot went down to the beach. It stood there, near the children and the dog, for about ten minutes.

Then, extending its claws, it dug a hole. A neat, square hole about thirty centimeters on either side.

Then it trotted back, settled back into power-saving mode.

Morag watched Seamus for a good few minutes, speculatively.

She didn't know why it had done that. Was it in response to some perceived threat? Some long-buried routine?

But then again, why did humans do things?

Seamus had defensive modes, threat modes, patrol modes. Some situations put it on guard, others got it to play football. But Morag couldn't say how that was different to human beings, when it came right down to it.

And digging holes for no good reason, using limbs built for climbing and defense to make something with no obvious use, was something very like human beings.

"I know what I have to do," she said to the robot.

Morag went back to the chief archivists the next day. Or, more precisely, she went back to John. The other two were apparently off about their various jobs about the archive.

"I can't do it," she said to him.

John didn't seem surprised. "You think Seamus is sentient?"

"No," she said. "But the fact is, *I don't know* if Seamus is sentient. And because I don't know, I can't dismiss the possibility."

John nodded. "There's always a place for you, and for Seamus, here at the archive if you change your mind."

So, Morag took her walking stick and set out along the Portmeirion Road, or the Pen-y-Groes road if that was how you wanted to think of it. Her robot by her side, the sun overhead.

She wasn't sure she'd made the right decision, or if Zeb and Dai and Maya would understand why she'd made it. She wasn't even sure how to tell them about it. What they'd say when she did.

But, whatever happened, she'd stand by it.

She heard footsteps hurrying behind her and turned. Maybe she'd left something behind at the glassworks and Nancy had found it.

But it was Saoirse. Her jacket flapping behind her, her head bare and her short red hair flying untidily in the sunlight. Her cheeks red from exertion.

When she reached Morag; she simply handed her a folder of papers.

"I looked it up," she said. "It took me a while, but I found it out. The thing they used to control asthma was called corticosteroids. That's the top document."

Morag took the folder. "And the rest of the documents?" She glanced at them. Careful handwriting on pieces of paper, small sketches.

"It turns out steroids are a thing you can stimulate the body to produce." Saoirse moved them off the road, not that anyone was particularly using it at this time of day. "I did some research, and this is a list of plants and other things that can be used to stimulate steroid production." She looked a little embarrassed. "I don't actually know how many of them work. If any. Some of it might be just urban legends. I got some of it from books about bodybuilding. But some of it's from medical texts."

Morag didn't quite know what to say. "Well, it's as good as anything we can provide, and it's certainly better than what we had before, which was nothing. You're not going to get into trouble for this, are you?"

Saoirse looked surprised. "Oh, heavens, no," she said. "I did the research, so it's mine to give away if I want."

"So . . . that's how it works? Then why were they asking me to give them Seamus?" Morag was confused, and angry at the same time. If they thought they could take advantage of her like that . . .

"That's how it works," Saoirse confirmed. "Everyone owns the archive. If you do a piece of research with it, that research is yours, and you can do what you like with it. That's what they were offering. Either you get them to do the research for you, by giving them Seamus, or you come here and do the research yourself. But you have to join the community to do that."

"I think I understand," Morag said. "Not entirely sure I like it, but I understand."

Saoirse's face softened. "Do please come back," she said. "Not now, not if you don't want to. But it would be good to have your knowledge, your mind, in the community. You don't have to stay forever. But it might be a good thing to do for a little while."

"And I wouldn't have to give them Seamus?"

Saoirse looked ambiguous. "I'm sure something could be negotiated."

Morag nodded.

"I don't think it's for me," she said. "Not right now, anyway." It would be many years before she left the farm, and she didn't know what she'd be wanting then. Or what Seamus would need. It wasn't a bad thing to have options.

"But my niece. I think she could get on very well in a place like this. Once she has these." She gestured with the folder. She could see Maya, once she had the protection, going through the archive, researching these corticosteroids. Maybe joining those little groups on the beach or in the square.

Saoirse smiled. "Then tell her we'd be glad to have her."

Morag nodded a goodbye, and carried on down the Portmeirion road. Her stick in her hand, her folder in her other hand, and her robot beside her.

She couldn't say why, but she had a feeling like she'd won.

ABOUT THE AUTHOR

Fiona Moore is a a BSFA and World Fantasy Award finalist, writer and academic whose work has appeared in *Clarkesworld, Asimov's, Interzone,* and five consecutive editions of *The Best of British SF*. Her most recent non-fiction is the book *Management Lessons from Game of Thrones*. Her publications include one published novel and one forthcoming novel; numerous articles in journals such as *Foundation*; guidebooks to *Blake's Seven, The Prisoner, Battlestar Galactica,* and *Doctor Who*; three stage plays, and four audio plays. When not writing, she is a Professor of Business Anthropology at Royal Holloway, University of London. She lives in Southwest England with a tortoiseshell cat which is bent on world domination.

In Which Caruth is Correct
CAROLYN ZHAO

You're not meant to fix what happens in the time loops. Doctor's orders, and that comes even before they give you the survey and the spiel and the confidentiality speech. The psych fiddles with his tablet in his cozy, yellow-couch office, and talks to you in a very grave and condescending voice. The tone checks out. What doesn't check out is how young you are, and how long this is meant to take.

"One year with meds and therapy," he says. "One month if we do a more interventionist approach. Take some time off work. I'll write you a note."

"Sure," you say. You can't take time off work. There's a client who's a nut, the project's on optimizing company debt (the good kind,) which is funny considering all your college debt (the bad kind,) and you're hoping the psych won't talk about billing, just forgets it somehow, but come on. Don't kid yourself. He absolutely will.

The psych gives you a sympathetic look. He's reading you wrong for the first time in the session.

"Just be safe and close them up," he says. "They're just memories, in the end."

Some Yale professor came up with it first. Trauma as a return to a point of singularity. Except, of course, the theory didn't account for how everyone had multiple loops, not singular, which meant there had to be multiple break points in a life. Multiple folds of time.

But the much more important, much more deliciously sensitive second problem was that no one could really agree on what trauma meant. The word had leapt into the English lexicon somewhere in the 80s, and all of a sudden everyone was pasting it on psych journal headlines, and then quoting it on Google searches, and then labeling it on Discord channels.

And the theorists said: well, there's feminine trauma and POC-trauma and poverty trauma, but it's only understandable if you have the Right Kinds of Words to talk about it.

And the therapists said: actually, it's about BPD, ADHD, PTSD, c-PTSD, all treatable with EMDR and CBT and DBT, but only if you have the Right Kinds of Money to pay for it.

And the influencers said: no, I'm traumatized because of X, Y, Z, and A, B, C, and you and I are too different except for when we're the same and not different, and have the Right Kinds of Feelings to have about it.

So there you go. Trauma of the everyday. Trauma of slavery. Trauma of the parents (always the parents,) but the truth is, time loops have been there since the start. People vanish into them. People never come back out. And it was a business guy who helped put the pieces together, after his wife vanished into a loop one day, because he followed her in.

They were caught in the morning where everything could have gone right. Breakfast on the table, sunshine through the windows, and their son preparing to drive off to school for the millionth time in a row. But what if his kid had taken a wrong turn that day? What if the driver hadn't run that light? What if his mother had begged and pleaded and sobbed and threatened and apologized and screamed and asked for him to stay home, please, please, just listen to your mother for once?

Well, she succeeded this time. Their son stayed home on the final loop. And that driver didn't hit him, and he didn't end up in a wreck of a Honda on the side of the road, tires spinning, classes missed, parents destroyed. And when his wife was holding their grumbling son for the first time in a decade, the business guy saw the singularity begin to close around them like an envelope.

He jumped back out. She didn't follow. And for the rest of *his* life, time loops appeared in the corners of his home, regret after regret after regret. And even though he took all the pills he could, and said all the therapeutic platitudes he needed to say, in the end, he walked into a loop, too.

So there, the case studies said. It's the trauma.

And it all makes sense. But the only thing you think about as you buy thirty dollars' worth of meds, and call up the tempo-therapist on the thick white card, and watch yet another singularity coalesce next to your dying houseplants, weird and swirling like someone's stirring the air with a stick, is how much work you're going to fucking miss.

And what to tell your dad.

The crazy thing is, you're not from a terrible background. You had one parent who's a lawyer and another parent who's a biologist-turned-homemaker, and sure, you were bullied for reading too much in class, and for wearing a ponytail so low it made you look like a Founding Father, but that's small stuff. That's daily-life stuff. They didn't even make fun of your home-cooked Chinese lunch in school.

Seriously. They didn't.

So it's not actually a surprise when you touch the first singularity, the one hidden underneath a jumble of folded clothes, and find yourself transported into your nine-year old body, which has just been stuffed into a brown paper tunic and had a mustache drawn across its face.

You're in a Birth-of-Jesus play. You're the Roman Guard threatening the defenseless infant-savior. You're at that perfect precipice of childhood where you're not quite *why* you don't want to go onstage, but the applause is dying down, the lights are coming on, and you are totally about to learn, for the first time, what the phrase "abject humiliation" means.

"Shit," you say, and take a step back and call your therapist.

Her name is Kelly. She walks you through it. You swallow two pills, step onstage, and focus on the present: her firm voice through the speaker and the aftertaste of sour plum juice in your mouth.

And it goes well. You say the magic phrases, you focus hard on sour plums, and the time loop dissolves around you like a—well. Like a bad memory. You're left standing in your bedroom, feeling stupid, smelling acetone on your lip, and holding a plum juice bottle in your hand. You're shaking, too, leftover stage-jitters. But you're not meant to fix things. It isn't meant to be perfect.

"I'm so proud of you," Kelly says when it's done. "I just wanted you to know that."

And if you were any other Asian kid with parental issues, you'd tear up now because no one's ever been proud of you, ever. It's the curse of the continent. The black magic brought over the border. Thou Shalt Never Know Thy Parent's Validation, big carved Chinese letters, commandment number eleven.

But that's not true. Dad's said "I'm proud of you" plenty of times. So you're just another Asian kid with a consulting job and an okay life, and so you say, very normally: "Thanks. I'll call you if there's another."

"Here when you need me," Kelly says, kindly, and lets you hang up first.

Back when you thought you wanted an English degree, you wrote a paper on textual singularities. The course talked about how there wasn't a word for "trauma" back in the day, and so people just went around calling things a "calamity." Floods? A calamity. Fires? A calamity.

Memories of a husband who died in the war? Also a calamity. Calamity this, calamity that. What was once a calamity becomes the everyday. What was once a flood becomes a ceaseless rain.

And in the poem you studied, the narrator lay in bed, mourning her lost love. Maybe she was in a loop. Maybe she was not. But it did rain every day, and it did not stop.

You linked it back to time—argued that the structure of the poem was a loop in itself. That grief made time spiral, made it a non-linear entrapment of the bio-social past. Read enough books and you can tell a story about anything, including what happens in a singularity. But in all the scientific papers, a singularity is a single point: no start, no end. The zeroth dimension, complete unto itself.

A place where time approaches eternity.

You visit your Dad on the second week of meds. They haven't affected you much—just made the singularities easier to see, so you don't trip over one when you're brushing your teeth or something.

Dad takes the news badly. Dad lives in a second-story walkup that he wishes was on the first story. Dad keeps a single cactus alive that you gave to him on his fifty-fifth birthday. Dad's had three people in his family (your family, you guess,) vanish into time loops. It was the third-leading, non-natural cause of disappearances in the Revolution and the Famine, because people simply walked into the loops and didn't come back out. Entire families vanished overnight for the chance to live without regrets. And there was no tempo-therapy back in the day, so it begins when Dad says, in Chinese:

"Oh no! Meds?"

"It's fine, Dad," you say. "I just did my first session with them last week. The Jesus play. Remember that?"

"I don't care about some Jesus," he says.

"America's a religious country," you say. But still, Dad's shuffling around now to clean up the couch for you to sit on. He doesn't talk about his sister, or your grandmother, but when there's tea on the table, and hawthorn candy in your mouth, he says, quietly:

"Is it something I did?"

"God, Dad," you say. "No."

"It was your Mom's birthday recently."

"And?"

"I worry about her," he says. "She's threatened to go into a loop before."

"Dad," you say, "I am not going into this," and he gets the message and stops talking. But he's silent for the rest of the evening, doesn't even play cards with you and his girlfriend at the end of the night. He just sits on the couch and eats hawthorn candy. Soon he starts wiping his eyes. And yep, that's your cue—you get up and pull on your jacket, and shut the front door without force, and for the entire way back, you try not to think about how he's more concerned about your Mom going into a time loop, and not you.

Not that you will, of course. But it's the misplaced concern that aches. And that night, when you get back to your fifth-story walkup in New York, New York, baby, of course you open the door to a singularity on the table, tilted towards you like a welcome home.

This one's beautiful. It's thin on the bottom and widens up to a tessellation around the top and center. You paw around for your phone and hit dial as you admire it from the doorjamb.

"Hey there," Kelly says. "Another one, then?"

"Yeah," you say. "This'll be quick, I hope," and you touch the tessellation and blink away tears, and this is it: your first breakup.

You're disappointed. You thought you were over this already. But nope, it's definitely prom night, and you're definitely sitting next to each other under the stars, empty bleachers over the football field. You rented this dress with a service online. You did your hair in a bun for once. And he's driven over from the local college to dance with you all evening, lights, disco, action, and to tell you at the end that he's been cheating on you.

"She's from your class?" you ask stupidly.

"Yeah," he says. "I'm sorry. I also think college just changes you, logically."

So there's the singularity. That one sentence. You're still a kid. So is he. But you're also about to punch him, you're about to stab your high heel through his foot, you're about to cry and scream and do some very illogical things, just to show him what's up, female rage, when Kelly says, into your ear: "Take a deep breath and count to three. Do not fix the loop. Accept it as it is. This is what happened. This is in the past."

And you do it. You count to three, through your teeth, and High School Boyfriend disappears into the stars behind you both. He doesn't deserve that kind of metaphor. But what the hell, you read too much anyways, and Kelly's voice talks you down, and you're back at your doorjamb sobbing into your sleeve as the tessellation dissolves into nothing, and you realize what the shape reminds you of: the flowers he bought you on prom night.

So that's why tempo-therapists are on your speed-dial. They talk people off the edge. They're very good at what they do. And since the introduction of tempos, time loop disappearances have gone way down. But tempo-therapists are tough to train, and not all cultures think time loops are about trauma this, calamity that. So it makes sense that China doesn't have them yet. It makes sense your Mom wouldn't be seeing one, either.

It goes like this:

You get the news at a conference, two years after you're done with meds and reality's settled back into its familiar groove. Mom's vanished into a time loop, Dad says over the phone, and he's crying for the first time in years, sobbing so hard he can't speak. You excuse yourself from the presentation, knowing your thesis advisor's going to be quietly disappointed in a "this really can't happen again" kind of way, but Dad's crying, your hands are cold, and all you can think about is: I wonder what she saw.

I wonder what she saw. I wonder what she regretted. I wonder what she wanted to fix so much that she threw away everything after the divorce and her kid not talking to her and her parents dying when she was eighteen, and just walked straight into the zeroth dimension.

You can guess, but it seems disrespectful to assume. Maybe she's alive, and she's happier than she ever was. In any case, the funeral's held on a mountain, where two of your grandparents and three of your great-grandparents are buried, and you make the flight there and lay flowers on her grave. It's empty, of course. But Dad's there, and he's crying, and it just fucks you up completely to see him cry, and so you bow.

You bow three times. You kowtow nine times. You place ten white chrysanthemums next to your mother's vertical, gold-carved name. Your dad asks you to speak at the funeral. You tell him you're tired from jet lag. But the truth is you both know that she wasn't a great Mom. And that's all you remember about it.

It takes a while for the next few loops to close. Sometimes it doesn't work, and you find yourself standing there like an idiot, wrist-deep in a singularity, your throat tight and hot, and Kelly says: "Make yourself a warm drink! We'll try again another day."

So you do, and you do, and the work hiatus goes on. It's not a good feeling. You lie in bed thinking about loops and floods, the snow coming down and sleeping in drifts on the street outside, and your job keeps tick-tick-ticking without you. All those worker bees on the clock; all that motion. You need to go back soon. Your debt weighs on you invincibly, crushing you flat, but going back to consulting feels like dragging yourself into a grave. It feels like never drinking chocolate again, never reading poetry again, and so you grab your laptop and start applying to other jobs. Any jobs. Please, oh please, dear fucking God, and then you land on the idea of graduate school, law school, medical school, but all of that seems even more ridiculous.

And besides. Debt is debt.

You talk to Kelly about it one night, and her voice echoes through the phone. "You're reliving mistakes happening before your eyes. The desire to fix things doesn't go away, so you're applying it to your life, right now. It's the most normal thing in the world."

"But what if this becomes a loop in the future?" You ask. "What if I never get out of this later on?"

"Do you think that will happen soon?"

"Well," you say, and "Maybe."

"Okay," she says. "I'm going to ask you to qualify that 'maybe.' "

She does. You do. The answer's all garbled up, but she drags it out of you eventually, like back when you thought you actually had a chance at med school, or back when you put on makeup for the first time and your Dad laughed, or back when the family dog died in China when you were still in the States, because you weren't ever going back to Beijing, not ever. The little guy slept at the door of your empty bedroom for five years straight. He never gave up on seeing you again, and oh, now that's regret.

You get through it all in one go. You're a wreck by the time she's through. So she tells you it must be hard. So she tells you your feelings are valid. So you hang up and open up your camera roll, and spend a long time looking at the photo of your dog gumming on an orange dinosaur toy, and then you cry so hard that your lungs ache. You were the one who gave up. He waited for you for the rest of his life. If only you hadn't been such a coward about going back, maybe he'd be alive, because you would've paid for any vet. You would've given anything to go back.

The sleep, when it comes, is in fits. The grief comes in dredging waves. And when you wake up the next morning with your eyes swollen, all the pain numbing you from the inside out, you compose and write a clipped little email to tell Kelly you've found another therapist, and you're switching to them instead. Pushing past boundaries is inappropriate. You weren't a good fit in the end. Anyways, thanks for everything, wish you well, best-regards, signature here.

Of course, it's a lie. You haven't bothered to look. But Kelly emails back asking for a session to clear up misunderstandings, and you shift-click-delete, and congratulations! That's that. So you buy yourself a drink.

You call work and tell them you're coming back. You go to work and pay off your bills, and just when you start feeling peace for the first time in months, the singularities start popping up all across your apartment.

The couch twists into itself. The walls come sliding to the floor. In the end, it's only by luck that your Dad visits one day, and catches you stepping into the swirl that's taken over your closet. Your dog always liked messing with your socks. You can scratch the little guy's chin if you reach out. He licks your hand, eyes filled with the irrepressible happiness of seeing you at last, and he'll never sleep outside your door again. You'll get it right this time, you'll never have to say good-bye, but then Dad's dragging you back out of the singularity, his grip crushing your wrist.

"*Baobei!* No!"

And you say "Yeah, I know," and then "Stop, I'm fine," and then you start crying, which causes him to say, "Think of your poor dad!" which causes you to cry harder, and oh, boy, here it really comes.

He says: "How could you do this?"

And "You were never like this when you were small."

And "What do you want to eat tonight?"

And "Your Mom really does love you."

And you say: "What in the fuck does this have to do with Mom?"

"Sweetie!" he says. "Don't say that," and you both listen to your sobs. Your dad's sixty-three years old this year. Your dad keeps hawthorn candy on his tea table just in case you visit. Your dad survived the Revolution and the Famine and has never had a time loop appear in his life.

You sit down. He boils hot water for you both. You drink it, and let the real apology unstick from your throat. He tells you he loves you, and the next day, he shows up at your door with paper towel rolls and a spare lamp because he thinks your eyesight is getting worse, and takes you to the library the way he did when you were a kid.

You borrow two books. You borrow ten books. You borrow so many books you guys can barely get them up the stairs in one trip. And it's all the stuff you've wanted to read for ages: Keats and Rilke and Lao She and Marquez, and you spend your weekends and your weeknights burning through the pages. You're looking for a kindred spirit. You're looking for someone to understand. And they get it, they all do, but it's Wikipedia that tells you that Keats was depressed for most of his (very short) life. Keats never lived happily ever after with his one true love. And Keats actually died of tuberculosis, not a time loop, and if you think about it, the reality is: most people don't succumb to a loop.

Walking into a loop is an active decision.

Walking into a loop is the fifth-highest cause of disappearances in the U.S.

And walking into a loop isn't a disease of weakness. Not really. It's a disease of pain, of conviction, of regrets so deep, you have to believe, full-heartedly, that you can fix things. You have to believe in it more than you believe in yourself. More than you believe in reality.

If only things could be better.

If only.

So you read about Keats again. You read about time again. You laugh at the language he uses, and you cry a little more, maybe for the girl you used to be, and maybe for all those years you can't remember as a kid, where all you knew was how to read poetry on the school bus and hope that going home that day wouldn't hurt so bad. And when the next singularity appears, you go down the list of approved NYC tempo-therapists on Temporality Today. You pick a handful who are POC. You call them with your good-patient voice. And when you find one who doesn't talk down to you, or pretend they have more degrees than they do, or panic when you stay silent just to see what happens, you walk up to a singularity and try again.

And it's not fast. It's even less fun. But when you think of stanzas instead of numbers, and mutter through poetry as the loop flows into and over you, waterfalls into rivers, your therapist isn't lying when they say you're doing what works. They hope you can talk to your Dad more. They hope you can read more poetry as well.

It still feels too personal to disclose. The dog, the Keats, and the calamity-singularities of it all. But they're not wrong. You hope so, too.

"Sure," you say. "I can do that. Reading poetry."

And it is poetry, really. Because the thing about singularities, or time loops, or trauma cycles, is that no one wants to know what you want to take back. It's weird. It's private. It's all the things you thought would never get to you.

So you've got to make some meaning out of it all. Delve deep into your guts and pull it all out, flip the interiority of pain on its head. And what you're doing is rearranging it, letting others witness the strange private pain of it, because that makes it public and therefore real. Maybe that's what the tempo-therapists are; maybe that's what loops do for your life. They force everything out into the open. It's just an eternal witnessing, a private calamity made public, then dissipating into everyday until—there's nothing you want for at all.

Really. Nothing.

Nothing but the sky above you, a strong blustery blue, when you're a normal Asian kid in Beijing, which is where you maybe-not-really-somehow belong, and when all you want to do is read poetry on the school bus, or chase your dog with your Dad, and drink sour plum juice from a big glass bottle without the taste of rain.

The last loop appears when you're slipping on your snow boots, on the fifth week of treatment. You're looking at applications to graduate school for literature, you're hanging onto your job by the fingernails, and it is, beyond all belief, Chinese New Year. Your Dad's cooked some egg dumplings for dinner tonight, a homemade Revolution recipe, and you're just about to grab your keys when you see it.

The singularity shimmers. This one sits on the floor, like a puddle, which could've been a nasty surprise if you stepped into it socks-first. You pocket your keys and consider it. You're off project tomorrow, and the loops are closing quick. There shouldn't be many left, and so you hit dial and press the hot screen of your phone to your ear.

"Good evening," your tempo says. "Let me know when you're ready."

Yes, you say, definitely ready, and you pop a hawthorn candy into your mouth, you step into the puddle with your boots on, and then you're back home.

Oh, you knew this was coming. It's part of every Asian American kid's story, isn't it? The real home. The big return-to-sender. The food-as-a-metaphor-for-parental-love kind of beat. You could say more, but actually—you just want to take it all in.

China. Beijing. The kitchen. Everything is as you remember it: the luminous blue wok open on the stove, the pebbled plastic refrigerator with its Disney stickers, the bottles of chili and vinegar standing like chess pieces on the countertop. Red clay powder sits by the sink. A hot water machine huddles next to the toaster.

And your Mom is standing by the stovetop, stirring a small pot of chopped cabbage.

She's wearing a red checkered apron, and her hair is the same bun as yours. This isn't the last time you saw her, not really, but it's certainly one of the last. You had a huge fight over this, absolutely cataclysmic, right before you left for the airport—but hey. This isn't that moment. This is a good moment. One of the few good moments you've had with her in your life.

"If you add sugar and salt," she says in Chinese, without turning around, "the cabbages release their juices, and there's no need to put water in."

"Really," you say. "That's so cool."

"What do you mean, cool?" she says. "Stop standing around and taste some already."

You walk up to the stovetop. You taste the cabbage leaf at the end of the long chopsticks, and you don't look at her face. You know what she looks like. Why remind yourself of it? Your tempo's talking into your ear, but you know the spiel already. So you do the whole mindfulness thing, make sure you're still wearing snow boots, thank them profusely, and tap the hang-up button on your phone.

You chew and swallow the cabbage.

"There," your Mom says. She's proud of herself. "How do you like the taste?"

You think about it. You taste cabbage and hawthorn and too much salt and sugar. You can't say anything bad, really, because she's sensitive to that and you want this good moment to last forever. There were so few of them with her. So rare, they were singularities. Twenty-five years of daughterhood and motherhood, all gone, subsumed into something you can't even bring yourself to remember, nothing you can ever fix, and all you have is this one little loop together, puddling on the carpet over your square-tile New York floors.

The tiny kitchen. The cold ashy Beijing air. The limestone crusts on the bottom of the glasses. The stupid fucking cabbage.

It's like reading poetry on the school bus. You just keep doing it, and you keep believing you're going somewhere better than you were, somewhere far away, but sometimes you'll come back to the same spot on the page, and the words be there like they always were.

"Well?" your Mom asks. She's getting impatient like she always does.

"I like it fine," you tell her.

And it's seriously the truth.

ABOUT THE AUTHOR

Carolyn Zhao is a med student, speculative fiction writer, and retired English major based in NYC and Chicago. Her work has been published in *Clarkesworld*. She loves her dog almost as much as her dog loves her.

The Brotherhood of Montague St. Video

THOMAS HA

At first I thought something had broken in my book.

I didn't notice until the afternoon light from the windows began to recede. I tried to increase the brightness settings of the page, but no matter how I thumbed the margins, they would not change. For the first time, I looked carefully at the gold printing along its spine. The book was dead.

What kind of library carried a dead book? I wondered.

No one responded to my calls for assistance. There were no working service-buttons near the shelves that I could see. I walked downstairs to the circulation desk. No one was present at the self-checkout stalls, and I assumed, like all other recent changes, that this was the result of cuts to the city budget.

The more I looked at the gold-laden book, the more I considered it may not have belonged to the library at all. It had no identification tag on the inside cover, no chip at its base. Perhaps someone had left it, hidden among the other inventory, for some unknown reason. There was no way to scan a book that didn't belong there, so I put it in my coat without checking to see if cameras were hovering over me and walked out the door.

The entire ride on the 2, I wondered if something would happen. I waited for an officer to pull me aside at the station exit. Or for a street drone to make me step away from the pedestrians on the icy sidewalk. But nothing came of it, my taking away the dead book. I was surprised, and even disappointed, in the nothing that seemed to follow.

"*The Winter Hills* by Carrigan Salt."

The owner of the video store studied the binding, the page edges, much as I did before. Alaric had an eye for dead things that I did not, and he understood instinctively the rarity of what I had brought him.

In the weeks after my mother's funeral, I had come to the video store more often, bringing boxes from her Court Street apartment. Recorded-over VHS tapes, floppy disks, and undeveloped photo rolls. The Brotherhood on Montague was always eager to collect physical effects and would accept donations of any kind, I had been told. Even if they could not use or preserve them, they often had a sense of who could.

I was curious if he would buy the dead book from me, given his obvious interest.

"I'll consider it." Alaric paused, then he redirected the conversation to my mother's things. Some of her belongings I had chosen not to donate outright. One in particular, I had requested the Brotherhood try to restore and copy.

"The digital video disc, the DVD, you asked about—we'll need a 650 nm red laser to create a copy from the scratched original."

"Just as it was? No optimization?"

It was important to emphasize this. Every other data center had been unable to pull the file without automatic edits to the image settings and content.

"That's right." Alaric nodded. "No optimization. Just as it was. The Brotherhood's burner is on loan. It'll be a week or two."

He was about to give back the dead book, but he kept touching the textured cover. "I never read this, the original, in ink on pulp," he said. "It's part of Salt's Long Wanderer series."

"Oh," I said, as if I had heard of it before. Salt's name had been vaguely familiar to me when I plucked the book from the library shelf, but if there were more volumes like this one, I didn't recall seeing them.

The old man turned several pages. He was reading, but it was apparent that he was thinking of other things. I could feel his mind split between the words and wherever else he was. His breathing slowed, and then he closed the book and put it in my hands. There was some sound in a distant part of the shop, behind the shelves and stacks of preserved things—spinning racks of cassette tapes, mounted pinhole cameras, an old standing arcade cabinet. A rhythmic rustling, there, that continued until I left.

Elii met me at the promenade after dark, not far from Montague.

We sat on a bench and watched the East River behind the slow-moving bodies on the walkway. I tried to show her the dead book, and she thumbed the margins before giving up when it wouldn't brighten. It was clear she had no interest in the thing.

I'd been hoping after several months of dating we'd be able to take off our amp-glasses, but she insisted we keep them on. I'd already snuck little peeks of her around the edges of my frames. I knew she did not look all that different without her themes. Her cheeks were less contoured, her lips less plump. The alterations in the glasses were only slight. Nonetheless, she had only ever let me take them off when we were in total darkness together. For people who kept glasses on, it was never really about looks alone.

She asked if I was almost finished with my mother's apartment. There were just a few more boxes, some paperwork, and the deposit to get back. My bereavement leave was done, and I had borrowed from next quarter's vacation time. But I'd be back in my apartment soon.

We began talking about the scratched disc I'd sent to Montague St. Video, how it contained, among other things, old footage my mother had shot and saved. Clips of us up at Lake George in the years after my father had left. I offered to show Elii some of it once it was restored and copied.

"It sounds like your mom held onto a lot," she said. "That's a lot to go through and settle up. A lot of things."

"Right. That's true. It is a lot. A lot of things. Too many, even."

"Yes, maybe too many," Elii agreed. "I was thinking, because there's so much, we should probably hold off on visits and videoconnects—until you're done settling everything, at least."

"Oh? I mean, sure. That does make sense."

"It just seems like something you should finish first. Don't you think?"

"You're right. No. You're right. I should focus and finish. That does make sense."

"Sorry again. For your loss."

"Of course." I went back to watching the dark glass and cement shapes of the city across the river instead of her, already half-forgetting whatever it was that we were saying. "I appreciate that," I said. "Yes, I appreciate that. I do."

Later, in the stillness of my mother's apartment, I began reading through more of *The Winter Hills*. I sat in her old chair, her scarf still draped over the arm and barely brushing against the rug. Lost in the pages, much as I'd been in the library.

Carrigan Salt's protagonist, the unnamed rider, rode his gray horse across flat and rocky lands and through sparse little towns. The character had a peculiar way of going from one place to another without a sense of purpose. In any other book, I would have known the shape of the narrative at this point. But not here.

He did not understand the urgency with which others lived. They all seemed so eager to reach a conclusion, no matter how partial or incomplete, but in his mind there were always more questions forming like eddies in a stream. Every town the rider visited, he liked to ask himself these three things: What is it these people want? What is it these people need? Are they striving toward one, or the other, with what they do each day? And in examining these things he usually came to a clearer understanding of the people in that particular place.

I fell asleep reading about thundering horses and cattle and sizzling heat. Outside, the heavy trucks on the BQE rattled the icy apartment windows, but I imagined them as hooves over hollowed rock. I dreamt of a man on a gray horse standing at a lake, watching a mother and her young boy at the water's edge throwing rocks. I woke up crying for reasons I did not understand.

My days had already lost normal proportion before the dead book. They were little eras contained within odd chambers that did not begin or end with a sunrise or sunset. There was the unlocking of my mother's online accounts. The post-funeral cremation and retrieval of remains. Notifying various agencies and sending copies of death certificates. Finding an attorney to settle any outstanding issues with her estate. The time spent reading *The Winter Hills* in meditative stretches felt no different. Just another era to add to the ones before.

Alaric had not yet finished with the disc I had given him on my next visit to Montague. I found him stooped over an album of postage stamps, carefully arranged on each page in airtight little sleeves. Behind him, a black-and-white movie played on a CRT, and a modified VHS player appeared to be recording the contents for the Brotherhood's archives. I asked Alaric, while he inspected the postage stamps, if the store sold any paper.

"As in, sheets? Uncoated? No pixelated surface? The Brotherhood has a relationship with the mill in Tarrytown, so we do have some supply, yes."

He did not ask why I needed it, so I assumed this was not too extraordinary of a request. I bought one ream with some store credit I'd accumulated.

My mother kept an old Trapwood typewriter she had gotten as a gift from her grandmother. She had shown me, when I was very young, how to replace the ribbon, but I still had to spend some time watching videos online before I could do it. Once I'd had everything, I put the copy of *The Winter Hills* next to me and began typing its words on the fresh paper.

The town was nothing like he knew. There was a solemnity to the way the miners at Copper Hawk lived. Their existence was like a duty they bore begrudgingly but also would not relinquish. The rasp of dust in their nostrils and mouths, the lines of their skin. They did not enjoy the brilliant bang of the white sun. It was only the swollen blackness of the shafts before them, and they could not remember what had been there before the mines had been birthed beneath them.

I didn't know why I'd begun this project of copying the dead book's text over onto fresh sheets. My day job as a freelance re-writer meant I often studied material like this. But typically I would be cleaning up inarticulate copy, trying to make output from some desk producer into something people could understand. My agency mandated simplified phrases and strict grammar rules we had to know by heart.

The Winter Hills did not have any of those phrases or rules. There were long turns that were not necessarily about efficiency or meaning, but about rhythm. It was a voice I wanted to transpose for myself to feel the words. I was getting lost in the book, but at a pace and flow that felt more like a dissolving comfort than the listlessness of despair.

It was also during those quiet days when I began to suspect something else was happening, especially when I left my mother's apartment.

Walking along the slushy sidewalk, past naked black branches waving like claws at the curtilage in front of the brownstones, I heard that distant sound, that rustling, I remembered from the shop. Not like soft wings, but something like plastic or the scrape of faux-leather.

There was a presence I could not explain.

I'd take breaks from typing and go down to one of the corner stores. No one would be working there in person, of course. The camera would dangle from tracks in the ceiling, following over my shoulder and monitoring every item I picked from the shelves. I'd scan my items at the self-check registers, and I'd think, for a second, that someone was in one of the aisles. But I also knew if I looked, I would be wrong.

The iron-handed sheriff of Copper Hawk did not take kindly to the rider or the differences between them. In his mind, every stranger was a new element to be carefully accounted for, and the sheriff was not one with the patience for it. He did not ask questions about what people wanted or needed, only what they could do. No, he and the rider were not the same at all.

The ending of the dead book was as mystifying as the rest.

The rider spent weeks in the mining town of Copper Hawk, slowly coming to the realization that the sheriff there, working under the auspices of a metals corporation, was bleeding the people of their wages and exploiting their labor. The last chapter involved a shootout, as these kinds of books tended to have. But instead of a decisive victory, the rider ended up winged and bleeding. The book finished with the rider, delirious, on his gray horse, barely escaping with his life out into the desert. Nothing resolved. No one in Copper Hawk saved. Perhaps the rider would return to the town and set things right in another book, but somehow I didn't get that sense. So the ending felt haunting, strange, and unfamiliar to me.

I found a living reprint of *The Winter Hills* for comparison. It was encased in shiny plastic, the spine with the usual rechargeable port. I scanned and skipped along the various digital chapters to see what had been altered by the publishers posthumously. It wasn't uncommon for the estate and rights holders to periodically update these kinds of stories. The benefit of a living book was that they didn't have to contact readers to update the content. Alterations would sync in the pixelated pages whenever the book went online next.

The biggest difference I noticed in the new electronic copy was the ending.

There was a shootout in Copper Hawk like before, yes. But instead of the loss and the blood and the shame of the rider, the iron-handed sheriff was the one to take a bullet. The miners of the town staged a revolt against the metals company in the third act. They set fire to some of the shafts with an explosion at the end of the action, to punctuate the triumph. I could almost sense the hand of audience-score maximizer programs in the plot. It could even have been a re-writer at my agency that oversaw the edition, for all I knew.

I felt better in some ways, having read the new, happier ending, but I forgot it promptly, like some garbled conversation I'd overheard on the subway, something that made me chuckle and then escaped my mind.

In my dreams, I kept going back to the image of the original ending—that rider bleeding, leaning over on his horse, clutching at its neck, and whispering softly to the beast. And then I remembered my mother wearing sunglasses, on a towel at Lake George, reading a magazine, while I ran back and forth on the white-hot sand.

"Why would they change it that way, *The Winter Hills*?"

Alaric was inventorying one of the last boxes of my mother's belongings. He held up a record and inspected its sleeve. There were also a series of digital postcards, rewritable electronic messages in thin plastic film, some from Cabo, others from Denmark, sent by my mother's younger sister who had never stayed in one place too long.

"People have a tendency to confuse change with improvement. So alteration seems like creation to some." The old man peered down the glasses dipping at the end of his nose. "We like the feeling of progress, and folks figured out a while ago that you can always tweak things in your surroundings to heighten a perceived movement through time. Even if, in truth, you haven't advanced anywhere meaningful at all."

"I don't know what that means."

Alaric laughed, to me or to himself, I could not tell. "I've never been accused of clarity." He typed something on his dust-covered computer and studied the digital postcards from my aunt. "It seems counter-intuitive, but it's really the preserved things—fixed markers that never move—that are the more meaningful measure of change. A traveler on the road can look at mountains, forests, other landmarks, and he understands the difference in his positions the farther along he goes. Just like when I listen to a song, look at a work of art, read a book. And then later, return to that same piece. Something will be different, will have moved, in me. That's the benefit of the work we do in preserving things in particular forms, I like to think. We remember who we were then, so that we know who we are now. Does that make a little more sense?"

His words did feel right. Like something I'd been thinking but didn't know how to articulate in the weeks of going through my mother's things. Again, I removed the dead book from my coat pocket and offered it tentatively to Alaric.

"Have you considered, by the way . . . " I felt almost embarrassed asking. "Whether you'll buy? The dead book, I mean."

He did not answer quickly. The question appeared to weigh on him. "I'm making inquiries, but I have to be frank. We may not be able to offer a fair price. Not what you could get elsewhere. We will do our best to get back to you soon."

"I understand."

"In the meantime, you should be careful."

"With the book?"

"With who sees it. Not everyone appreciates these things the way the Brotherhood does. Materials that can't be modified, adjusted, or updated. Some enjoy true things like that. Some can't stand them."

"I see," I replied, but again, he had lost me.

"Where did you find this copy, again?"

"Just an old place in the city. My mother used to go."

"Your mother . . . she was from this neighborhood, you said?"
The old man studied my face and the postcards, like he was trying to figure something out. But if he put anything together, he didn't say a word about it or give any other indication. After we'd finished with the box, and as I was about to reach the stairwell, he called out to me.

"West Nyack."

"Hm?"

"There's a Brotherhood in West Nyack," he said. "Not that far out of the city. They know dead books and sometimes teach others about them. If that sort of thing interests you, maybe those are the ones you should go and see. They might have something to offer or to teach you too."

I thanked the old man for the information. There were other things I probably should have asked, but that I just let go. I suppose I thought there would be time with other visits. I did not think too much then about leaving Montague St. Video behind.

Caliper John approached not long after that conversation. Or rather, he decided to make himself known, I suppose. Even then, I should have known he'd been listening for some time.

In the days that followed, typing and re-typing passages from *The Winter Hills*, I found myself awake in the quietest parts of the night. Sometimes, as my mother and I used to do when I was a kid, I made my way to a small Greek diner a couple of blocks from the apartment that was open at all hours. The owners had changed a couple of times over the years, but the kitchen stayed the same through each transition. No automated preparation. Just staffed by a few older men who rotated shifts. My mother had always gotten the fries and the coffee, oil and acid, she'd call it, and read at the blue booths closest to the radiators. So I took to doing the same on these chilly nights too.

He came to my table while I was reading, alone.

"Excuse me, but that book you have there. Have you ever considered selling? It's been some time since I've seen an original Carrigan Salt."

His voice was weak, almost a whistle, and did not fit, because he was so unnaturally large, bigger than any man I had seen. Something animalistic in my brain went off. I felt threatened by his shape and the way it towered above me. He wore tiny glasses and a tailored jacket, little signs of seeming gentility. But they could not obscure the physicality and power of his frame.

He introduced himself as Caliper John and said he had seen me reading *The Winter Hills* and felt compelled to come by. Later, I realized he did not specify when he had seen me reading the dead book.

I asked if he was with one of the Brotherhoods, and he shook his head. "Not quite."

His eyes would never rest for too long on the cover of the dead book, like he could not take in too much of its details. I noticed, then, a special watch on his wrist, running applications I could not read from where I sat. The watch was similar to mine and other personal computing devices, but it was clearly more expensive and technically advanced. This one seemed like a tiny bracelet on that beefy wrist, and yet he managed to tap and swipe at the watch's face and pull up several programs with ease.

"Physical depreciation might impact its value, but you could get quite a high price from specific collectors. For example . . . " A few taps into a search bar on the watch and he pulled up a store profile, which he projected just above the watch screen. An antiques and rare editions shop called Satoshi Print. It looked like it was somewhere on the Upper West Side, based on the address. "Just an example, you understand," he said.

"You work for them? Satoshi Print?"

The large man did not meet my eyes. He was listening to the sounds from the kitchen, the sizzle of a frying pan, or maybe the clang of utensils.

"I could make inquiries for you. This is, you understand, not the sort of establishment where individuals can approach. Mine is a tricky business with very little trust. But I am something of a known entity. So if I should broker something, they will make serious offers. It could be quite a lot. Potentially five or even six figures. And you and I could work out a percentage for my commission."

"I . . . I appreciate that. I'll have to think about it. Mister . . . "

"John. Caliper John."

"Right."

"Right." He repeated, not mockingly, but more like an uncontrolled echo. The large man, Caliper John, seemed to sense a need to adapt his approach with me, so he smiled. It felt practiced, and he appeared to think it would be reassuring. "People do not often hesitate when I tell them there is that kind of money involved. You understand what I am telling you, about the money involved."

"Sure. I don't know. I've grown attached, I guess."

"Ah. Grown attached. Yes." He touched his small glasses. "I understand what you are saying about growing attached. But items can be replaced. Similar ones bought. That is, after all, what all of the money is usually for. There is a substitute for everything. A meaningful replacement. Everything. You understand what I am saying too?"

He touched the strange watch, and something beeped on my own. I realized he had sent me his contact information, which now appeared on my watch display. I had not accepted any link or pairing, which was usually required for such transfers.

He was smiling, but there was something violative in that otherwise innocuous gesture. I realized he was showing me, in his own way, how insubstantial the separation was between us, and how easily he could pass through it, if, or when, he wanted.

The large man stood and buttoned his jacket around that swelling frame. "I will circulate this, on your behalf, and let you know if there is any interest. If I come back with a number, I ask that you please consider it seriously."

I looked away from his stare until he disappeared, and then I very slowly finished my coffee and fries. I wanted time to pass, to put more space between me and that man. I left my tip and thanked the kitchen and headed out into the cold. As I crunched on the sidewalk slush I felt it again, that hovering presence somewhere about, though I could not track it at first.

The rider felt an unsettling and restless quality to the iron-handed sheriff. There was a hollow in the man that went deeper than eyes could see. He did not operate outward from a source but took things from around himself to sustain an internal void.

Beside the trash cans of a nearby restaurant, I saw something move close to the ground, making that rustling sound. It went quickly, but from what little I could see, it looked like a lizard with hundreds of legs, and yet it was the size of a small dog. There were strange translucent wings up and down its back, rubbing against itself like plastic sheeting while its body undulated further into the darkness.

Between the shadows, I thought I saw its nearly human face staring out at me from behind one of the wet dumpsters, but I did not stay long enough to be sure.

What surprised me most was not the offer from Caliper John, but how it came.

Elii contacted me wanting to meet, not on videoconnect, but in person, despite our previous conversation. In fact, she chose a nice restaurant, next to the bridge and overlooking the East River—*Oubliée*. I told her that place seemed a little out of our reach, but she said that it was taken care of. I didn't have the presence of mind to ask her what that meant.

I only knew *Oubliée* was the type of restaurant that required a jacket and reservation and a certain demeanor. Everyone there was intentionally and strategically thin. The patrons who seemed uncomfortable and sharp-eyed and on their watches were likely of the working layer of the city. The ones who were slower and well-rested carried electronic notebooks like they were serious or artistic people, but leisure was clearly their business and everyone knew it. I kept thinking about the rider in *The Winter Hills*, his three questions, while we were seated and studying the menus, which seemed to have no prices.

What is it these people want? What is it these people need? Are they striving toward one, or the other, with what they do each day?

The waitstaff was clearly informed to take good care of us.

A young man came by with a tray of pills—relaxers and enhancers and different kinds of stimulants. The right elevating component could brighten flavor and become the perfect complement to a meal, I had always heard. Non-addictive. Neurotropic. Personally designed. If you could afford it, why wouldn't you? That was the implicit tenor when these things were presented.

Elii picked two bright blue pills the waiter explained had been manufactured in Fukuoka and would go well with the fresher ingredients on the menu tonight. I struggled with the decision but ultimately went with the yellows, which were supposed to be mildest.

Elii kept her amp-glasses on, and talked very animatedly about the food, which was some fusion of several cultures that I did not understand. At a certain point in the meal, though, it became clear that she was supposed to talk to me about the dead book. The dinner reservation, all of this, came about because she'd received messages from Caliper John.

"I'm actually not sure how he found me," she admitted. "I would've, you know, told him to pound sand, but he said he wanted someone you trusted to give you the number."

"Right." I drank some wine.

"It's a big number."

"Right."

She told me what it was, the offer for my copy of *The Winter Hills*, and it was, in fact, a big number. More than I could earn as a re-writer in a decade.

"I don't feel comfortable, to be honest."

"Selling?"

"Selling to him."

Elii closed her eyes, like she was feeling some pleasant effect of the meal. "Do you have another buyer?" She hummed. "One of those video stores, maybe they have some kind of offer?"

"No. That's not it." I shut my eyes too, feeling dizzier than I expected to feel. "I just don't get the sense that good will come of giving anything to that man. I don't know why."

"Well, he's just a broker. The buyer's someone he knows at Satoshi p—"

"Satoshi Print. Right."

The problem, of course, was that there was no Satoshi Print.

The large man had shown me its information at the diner. There were numerous corroborating sites, reviews, mentions for Satoshi Print I'd found since. But when I went on an early Sunday up to the neighborhood out of a percolating curiosity, just to get a sense of what kind of business this really might be, I found only a half-empty parking lot.

No, there was no Satoshi Print in the physical world to speak of. And if Elii were being honest, I think a part of her already could have guessed it too. This Caliper John and people like him using digital husks, they were not the type of people who usually meant well.

"I get it." She cleared her throat and tucked her hair behind her ear. "You don't like it. That kind of thing. The smoke and mirrors. Shiny and empty. Even if they paid you upfront—did I say he said he'd pay upfront? Anyway. You still wouldn't take it. Not you. Because you like things solid. Things to hold onto. Like the book. And so, you hold on."

"I guess that's right," I agreed. "Yes. Things like the book. I do prefer to hold on, at least, for a little while. Sure."

"Of course. For a little while." She nodded. "But not in the long run. You don't want to be that kind of person in the long run."

"That kind of person?"

"You know. With too many things. Didn't you say that, about your mother, how she held onto too many things? And you don't, you know, want to be too much like that."

I stopped eating, and Elii seemed surprised. I wasn't angry. I just couldn't remember if I had said that about my mother the other day. It sounded like something I would say, but I just didn't know anymore.

"Listen, I understand," Elii began again delicately. "Right now you've got something of value. Something that feels important. But nothing's all that important, when you get down to it, in the end. Books fall apart. Memories of books fall apart. Nothing is solid or lasts, right? Nothing. Not that and not us."

"No. Not us. That is true."

"So at least with the money—and it's a lot of money—you get to have some fun and enjoy. That's all I see when it comes to this. So long as he pays you first, I say you might as well go for it while there's an offer out there. Why hold onto something you know is going to end up as more nothing eventually anyway?"

Across from us, a couple laughed. The woman bent over and vomited quietly into a little silver pitcher with a lid and daintily wiped her mouth. One of the waiters came by discreetly and picked it up off the floor and took it away. Other customers seemed to have an easier time averting their eyes than I did, familiar with erasing unpleasant things like these.

The enhancers I had taken began to hit their full stride. My head felt like a gigantic bowl, expanding and curving and stretching. The music and dim lighting of the restaurant seemed untranslatable in my brain. But I kept thinking about what Elii said: why hold onto something you know is going to end up as nothing anyway?

Yes, I thought, there was some truth there: why?

At some point, Elii took me from the table and led me somewhere out into the cold with our coats. She said that there was more for the evening, that Caliper John had not just taken care of the dinner, but had set out more for us to see.

We rode together in an automated cab uptown, light flickering and streaming through the pristine plastic windows; then we were in a white marble lobby; then in a gold-colored elevator that was almost as large as my apartment, rising up to the top of a hotel.

Elii had a watch on her wrist that I did not recognize. It was sleek and well-fitting. She used it to swipe us through every scanner and walk-gate we passed in the area. I briefly saw IDs on one of the hotel screens for a "Mr. and Mrs. Uqbar." More digital husks like Satoshi Print, or were they real people, somewhere? I wondered but did not think about it for too long.

There were no employees at the front desk to verify anything. No one kept us from going up to the penthouse suite, so long as Elii's watch kept opening the doors. Each door after the other we just . . . went on through.

There was too much space between everyone now, and it was too easy to advance like this. That was how Caliper John did the work that he did, I knew. He and others like him, they were people who worked their way through all of this space.

From the suite's living room, I could look out and see much of the lower part of the city, everything unpleasant at a distance, small. This, too, like much of this evening, felt unreal. And I suppose that was part of the point of this, his point, and maybe Elii's point too.

What did any of it matter, if it came and went with so little effort?

"Wait," I said, before Elii's slender arm could reach to turn off the lights. "I just—I just feel a little woozy, and I want to take these off." I touched my amp-glasses and hers. The yellow pills were still spreading through my body like a kind of sickly heat, and I felt like I could almost see through the walls.

Elii did not say anything for a moment.

"Why don't we just—"

"No."

Her face went still.

"No?" I laughed. "But I thought—I didn't really think you would care. Nothing lasts anyway, right? I just want to—"

"No."

In the silence that followed I knew that something had shifted in Elii. She had spoken so glibly before, about the transience of everything. But maybe that was something she'd heard before or been told to say. This, on the other hand, was very much her. This thing she couldn't do, with the glasses, was real, and I could feel it. There was something in this that mattered. Something she could not share.

I was a little surprised, but I think I understood.

I couldn't explain, but I understood.

I told her so, too, before I left the hotel room.

Yes, that was something, for the first time the entire evening, I could understand. A reminder of something similar, in me, that I could not get rid of easily either. There were still real beliefs, in her and in me, that couldn't be reasoned out of existence, no matter what others told us. There were parts of us, still real, and remembering that was good. I needed to remember that. So that was good.

Outside of the lobby and back in the cold, I found that a rising unease had returned. It could have been the yellow pills taking a turn. But no, I could sense it elsewhere, and I was sure. The large man who called himself Caliper John was unhappy with the way things were going, the way I was withdrawing from what he had prepared. I felt again that presence that had been with me over the days and weeks. There, in the delivery drone that buzzed at 6th Avenue. In the red camera ball floating in the department store window. In every mechanized eye between here and the East River and beyond.

I touched the dead book in my coat pocket, its textured surface, and I felt even more certain than before. I had to make my way downtown and across the river, back to Montague Street. Whether the Brotherhood could pay or could not pay for the copy of *The Winter Hills*, I wanted to go to Montague Street with the dead book. They would know better what to do, I thought, because of the care they took with things like this. Better than me, and certainly better than Caliper John.

I swiped my watch at the handle of an automated cab at the curb, but it did not open. *APOLOGIES. A PROCESSING ERROR, MR. UQBAR,* the taxi's window flashed. Over at a store, I tried an ATM, but scrambled data or a bad connection kept me from completing the transaction. *UNABLE TO READ YOUR INFORMATION, MR. UQBAR. SORRY FOR THE INCONVENIENCE.* This was the opposite of what happened earlier in the evening. Someone wanted to show me how quickly these impediments could appear. Just a few changes, and I could not get where I needed to go.

The iron-handed sheriff made sure there was no welcome. No respite. Everything Copper Hawk did was done at the sheriff's instruction, and the rider could feel the town shifting away from him in every direction, no matter where he went.

When I was a boy, my mother and I used to play a game.

This was before the city had fully transitioned into an extended network. She had taught me how to look for the dead spots underneath stationary cams. How, if you could not avoid a stretch with monitors, to cheat your face at an angle so that programs had issues scanning you to completion. She knew that certain brownstones with a specific pre-war style were historic, and therefore adding machinery to their exteriors was not permitted. The alleys between them were best for cutting routes. Certain subways would probably never be fully up to date, because the infrastructure had been done a particular way decades ago and could not be changed without significant cost.

I thought of her, and all of this, when a four-legged police-walker trotted by, stopped, then turned in my direction. Something flickered across its head panel—the pixelated outline of a facial expression. I moved back and away, between two buildings across from the hotel, and down an unmonitored street that led to a service entrance to one of the older underground stations. My mother had shown me this one, years ago, when we had been caught uptown in the rain.

The tunnel below was empty, and I studied the mosaic tiles of one of the walls.

In the dark, a familiar rustle trailed behind me—a sound I realized had followed me long before Caliper John introduced himself at the diner. He'd been watching me since the video store, maybe the library, I realized, though I couldn't say exactly when it began. My mind was only now piecing it together, those hundreds of legs rubbing against translucent wings, the sound of a synthetic, plastic multi-limbed surveillance device, getting swallowed by a rhythmic scraping of metal and rumbling of *klak-klak-klak*ing of an incoming train.

I couldn't see it, that thing, whether it was below the platform or somewhere behind the stairs. But I knew Caliper John was in the remote device, within that little body, controlling and looking out. An empty shell where there was enough space for him to operate.

Flickering light spilled from the moving train windows as it pulled up to the platform, and I could see the lizard-body beginning to lean out from the dark. That face and neck hunching forward, extending itself out from that long shape with its little legs. The face had too many lines. Little seams where plating and pieces were fitted together to look like a person but could not quite pull it off.

The lifeless lens-eyes, like dark little bubbles, fixed on my coat, as though he could see through to the dead book in my pocket. And I could feel Caliper John fixating, so palpable and alien. Alaric had said there were people who despised materials like the dead book because they could not be conveniently compromised or manipulated or remade. I could see it. Caliper John did not want to acquire and preserve *The Winter Hills*. He only wanted to contain or destroy it, if given the chance, and I knew now I could not give him that chance.

I got onto the subway car before that shape could slither out further into the light.

In the rattling, turning, and bumping as the car pulled away from the shadowy station, that long thing withdrawing back to somewhere I could not see, I looked down at my watch, thinking again about how Caliper John had accessed everything within it. I placed it under one of the seats and left the train at the next stop, then got on the local train behind that one instead. It would take longer, but it would not be anywhere near where he'd be watching, I thought.

By the time I got back across the river and up onto the surface, I couldn't feel it anymore—the presence behind me. I clutched the dead book in my coat, and I kept thinking about dropping it through the mail slot of the video store, thinking it was just narrow enough, maybe, to fit its way through that slot.

The rider wanted no fight. But he also knew the sheriff of Copper Hawk knew nothing but. And for people accustomed to using violence, there was never going to be any other way. For them, it was a natural repercussion of moving in the world.

The two men shared a drink together from a bottle, as a courtesy. But the rider took very little. He was afraid of what sharing too much might mean. And he was no longer thinking about the people of Copper Hawk and their troubles, or about the people he'd met out in the flat country. He wasn't even thinking, really, about the blood and gunfire to come. The rider thought only a cold thought.

This might be it.

He had found nothing in the sands or the plains, nothing in the towns or settlements and farms that he'd seen that he could take to heart, and this might be it.

There were fire trucks gathered on Montague Street, splayed at crooked angles and with ladders raised. Men yelled at a deep blackness that barely hid a roaring sound, a rapid whirl of orange light that moved in and out of holes in the crumbling surface of a familiar building, pressing against the cold air like an animal beating against the bars of a cage, something wailed from behind the billows. I stood there on the street with others, knowing it was too late, and it was all gone.

Montague St. Video and everything that had been saved there, burning.

Decoupled and scattered into the smoke and air.

Everything I'd given of my mother to the Brotherhood.

Just smoke and air now.

Nearly all that was left of her, now just smoke and air.

I never saw Alaric after that. Never learned, with certainty, what had happened to the store. The news articles were vague, specifying neither casualties nor cause, though I had my beliefs. Still, somehow, despite the fire, the old man found a way to deliver what he had promised.

There was one last piece of mail from Montague St. Video in the lobby when I got back to my mother's apartment. I didn't know why he hadn't called me to pick it up, or when he had sent it. But it was there. The restored copy of the DVD, just like we'd discussed.

I used my mother's old laptop, one of the only things left in her otherwise empty place, and I watched the file. Not optimized like all the other copies I'd tried to make after she died. Not cleaned up so that I wasn't crying in it. Not edited so that she didn't have those dark circles under her eyes.

My mother looked tired. She had insisted on the getaway to the lake, recording it all, the way she liked to collect things. But she didn't know, in those early days, how to handle me without my father around. I could see the veins in her hands when she applied sunscreen in the video. A cigarette dipped in her lips. She was stretched out on a beach chair, trying to look calm, even though we'd been screaming at each other moments before the camera started going.

Right before she hit record, I had been asking her where dad had gone, why she'd been so mean about him, why he didn't want to come back to us, and she had slapped me.

It was sudden. And without the video, I almost wasn't sure it had happened. But it was there, minutes later, when the camera shifted in her hands and I came into view. I could see it in the aftermath on that little boy's face in the video, in the red almost-welt on my jaw and part of my neck. I recalled the bright sting, the hot tears spilling, no matter how hard I tried to keep them in. All those little things you wouldn't have seen if they'd improved upon the file. I watched her, how she was, exactly as she was back then, on the terrible lonely edge of something. And now, with less resentment, and a tiredness of my own, I felt it all.

The dark circles under her eyes, her hands, my burning face. Nothing lasts, Elii had told me. Nothing lasts, that was true. But I also didn't have to give everything up so effortlessly, the way everyone else did, either. Erasing the bad felt only a step away from erasing the good, and I just didn't have it in me to do that. Especially with the people I loved most of all.

My mother did what she could, and I did what I could, in the years we had together. So I wanted to remember as much as possible, even hurtful things—the oil and acid, the scarves, the games, Lake George. Because I knew I would never remember nearly enough. No number of discs or books or notes or typewriters or boxes sorted through and preserved would capture it all.

I would try, but I would never be able to remember enough.

Before I locked up, I wrote Elii a digital postcard like the ones my aunt used to send, telling her I was leaving the city for a short while. I hoped to see her when I got back. I didn't think we were done talking about what mattered and what was real. I don't think either of us really knew enough yet to know what mattered or was real. But maybe the next time we found one another, we would. Or maybe not. I supposed we would see.

The trip uptown, working my way around the cameras, I kept thinking I saw a large shape, much too big, following me from behind. Something like Caliper John would be there at a park bench, or at a bus stop, but then would be gone. Only able to do so much in the cold brightness of day.

I got to the bus station, cheating my face away from the self-checkout when I bought the ticket. I watched the gray highways rise and the glass disappear behind me. There were fewer cameras in the small neighborhoods and roads out in West Nyack; at a certain point, when I got to walking the main streets, there were none.

From the outside, the Brotherhood video store looked almost identical to its Montague Street counterpart. The color of the frame, the style of window, everything, like it had been plucked out of time. Alaric had said they taught others here. The idea of that, of maybe joining in remembering what was dead drew me to this place, and I kept thinking of a passage toward the end of *The Winter Hills*. The one I'd typed more than any other, from that ending that stayed in my dreams and mixed with memories of Lake George and the heat, the image of the rider slumped on the gray horse, bleeding and delirious as he wandered away from Copper Hawk.

He knew that the world was unspeakably broken and turbulent and ill-formed in its foundations, a violent and material realm, ever coming apart. But he had to believe that the pain and impermanence was a kind of lie. Because there was something buried within him, somewhere, and with it a feeling that even if he were to disappear some fragment would echo beyond this time and place. Yes, he told himself. They could take everything substantive from him, but not that. They would get many things from him, but they would never get that.

I stepped into the store and put down my bags. I could hear the slight clunk of my mother's Trapwood inside hitting the floor. I clutched that gold-laden dead book in my hands and walked to the counter, where an old man looked up at me.

He did not seem at all surprised.

"Come on in," he said. "Let's see what you've got."

ABOUT THE AUTHOR

Thomas Ha is a Nebula and Shirley Jackson Award-nominated writer of speculative short fiction. In addition to *Clarkesworld*, you can find his work in *Lightspeed Magazine*, *Beneath Ceaseless Skies*, and *Weird Horror Magazine*, among other publications. His work has also appeared in The Year's Best Dark Fantasy & Horror series edited by Paula Guran. Thomas grew up in Honolulu and, after a decade plus of living in the northeast, now resides in Los Angeles with his wife and three children.

The Texture of Memory, of Light
SAMARA AUMAN

As my implants processed and transformed the scene in front of me from moment to memory, the silky iridescence of an oil slick slid over my field of vision. With that wash of colors came a muted mourning, for I had caught the bronze glint of my mother's arm in the recycling heap outside one of the pawn shops that brokenly yawned on the streets of the Verd.

Can something so broken beckon? If so, its twisted frame called me forward with the solemnity of a funeral bell. I was weighed down already by guilt and mourning; the paperwork for her cremation lay crumpled in my workpack as it had for weeks. The flowers her loved ones had sent for the funeral had died, but I hadn't yet had the time or energy to dispose of them. But it was the very density of significance of that arm, its light roseate and yearning, that bent me down and had me collapse upon the sidewalk with the power of its gravity.

No mistake. I needed no memory implants to tell me that this was her. Hers.

The arm that she had adopted after the factory accident. An arm meant to double her strength and make her more efficient in her work, but in this light, it had a limpid beauty still. The metal scuffed and scratched with a thousand days of back-breaking, heart-breaking work. Its component parts showed the care, still, that she had put into all of her mechanical parts, though my implant muttered in my brain that many of those components were now obsolete, could never be replaced.

Oh, like she.

Though I had to awkwardly squat on the sidewalk among the crowds to do so, I reached forward and flipped it over so that its front plate lay exposed.

Scratched into it with my childhood's ambivalent malevolence was a lily-of-the-valley, its bell-shaped blossoms now tolling with a daughter's regrets. Finding this, touching this was a small miracle, one whose power words would never be able to drain and explain away.

The texture of this memory that I held in my trembling hands abraded away any thoughts of errands I had planned to complete that day; the texture of the light against this bronze miracle smoothed away the anxiety that prickled against me and allowed my tears to run uninterrupted down my face.

Boarding the South Line at Verdigris station meant that finding a seat for the journey back into downtown was painless enough; few people rode the train from this station to its cosmopolitan terminus. The moss-stained enormity of the Verd had a gravity that could not help but swallow its inhabitants as they struggled to breach the neighborhood's event horizon from its interior.

The train was emptier than normal on that day; perhaps the chattering of autumn's teeth and the emerging chill had convinced everyone to shelter indoors, their devices connected to their hard-fought, barely bought large screens that displayed their cozy games or raucous streams for the entire family to watch.

Family.

I had placed my workpack on the seat next to me, only for my mother's arm to push past its smooth flap and dangle its hand outside it. It bent daintily at the wrist, its palm facing down, from which depended splayed fingers. It almost seemed like it would spring to life like a child's automaton at a birthday gathering; some sort of prestidigitation seemed inherent in the curve of the fingers. Thus far, it had summoned only heartache, no rabbits or butterflies or pigeons.

My implant did not know how to read the emotions oscillating in my mind. A child's top about to tip over, a gyre about to spin itself out of its own orbit. One moment, a silvery sheen, the dangerous mercurial shine of a mirror's tain, overlay the image in front of me. The next, the bronze of my mother's arm intensified, recalling funeral masks and hereditary sorrows. Then the gold of afternoons that are meant to fade, meant to fade.

Memory is such a fragile thing, depending so sweetly as it does from the emotional framework of one's mind. A false or ambiguous or complicated sentiment can, like an errant breeze, shake reality from the blossoms of one's memory like morning dew. Even my memory implants struggled to keep pace with the quixotic nature of the human heart.

As the train slid confidently to its stop at the Green River Garden station, I gathered my workpack into my arms. I attempted to surreptitiously slip my mother's hand into its hiding place before the inevitable crowd sieved itself into the train car. Like clockwork, like efficient coding, the people of the crowd did as they were programmed to do and filled the car. In my emotional state, they were reflective specters, devoid of real meaning to me as individual people, but devastatingly effective at reflecting back the fear-of-not-being, the fear-of-not-belonging that I felt as I clasped my workpack to my chest. I watched their expressions and the hazy reflections in the train windows to make sure that my mother's arm did not pull itself out of my pack like a magician would their synthsilk scarves.

But I too was a specter. Only one person looked at me, and when she did it was not toward my workpack that she glanced, but at the hollows of my eyes. I could see her mouth moving between a commiserating frown and a faint smile. I shut my eyes, then, wary of attracting pity.

With my eyes closed to the light that my aesthetic implant used to shade and shape my memories, I felt the weight of my mother's arm more clearly. I felt its shape, sturdy and strong and sure. Despite it all, I felt the warmth of my mother's embrace.

With another half dozen stops to go before the train brought me home, I allowed myself the luxury of picking up one of the mirror-shard fragments of childhood memory, a memory formed before my implants could sculpt them into beauty for me.

For those of who adopted the Nimi implants, so popular then but less favored now, our memories of our pre-installation pasts exist only in scattered echoes, shadowed echoes of leaves stomped into the wet concrete of autumn's sidewalks. I had thought, when I spent my teenage and young adult years saving up for a Nimi implant, that it would act as fixative does on a graphite drawing, holding the illustrative dust of my memories in place. It was only years later that I realized that memory cannot be fixed. It cannot be pinned. My implant enhanced each moment I lived into a scintillating memory; it tracked the emotions I associated with every evanescent detail and built upon the trellis of my memory a new story, a new narrative that was more emotionally effective, more complete than any organic remembering. My graphic design work grew heavy with the plentitude of emotionally fruitful memory, and the success of my freelancing allowed me to build myself a steady life. A sturdy one.

But the memories of my life prior to the implant would sometimes fall apart in my hands. The scudding of waves breaking upon the shore, the fragments of a teapot that childish hands dropped on the kitchen tile.

Sitting in the train car that day, my mother's embrace a memory made concrete in my arms, I remembered. Partially. Regretfully.

I had run my fingers over the weave of this memory time and time again since my mother died. I was caught in the loop of it, the rhythm of it. This memory was becoming worn like an old blanket, with its texture becoming softer and its holes becoming more numerous every time I mentally passed over it.

This was a memory unglazed by the sensitivity and the emotive power of my implant. Raw and rough and incomparably painful.

In the months following my mother's injury—the one where she lost her flesh-arm—she came home late each day. I was a child. I didn't understand anything but the wanness of her face in the streetlight that leaked in from outside our bent blinds. One night in particular, my mother had bent over. Exhausted. She reminded me of a robotic vacuum left alone in a corner, unable to return to a place where it could recharge. My siblings were scattered among the rooms of the apartment, dealing in the quiet tragedies of their own lives.

I wanted . . . something. Something from her, probably.

What it was I can no longer remember. I remember only the anger. The tantrum trembling along my jaw and in my fingertips.

Still, she slept on.

I took Ivy's pen knife from among memory's hazy kitchen clutter. I carved it, my childish emblem, into my mother's arm. The same stem, the same blossoms that glided down so gracefully, like ballerinas gathering momentum for their pirouettes.

I had carved my disappointment into my mother's new flesh.

I refused to meet the eye of my neighbor as we and her designer dog (pit retriever? mastbull? terrordoodle?) boarded the elevator and skimmed along the height of our building to our floor. The dog sidled close to me and lifted the flap of my workpack with his nose; frightened, I abruptly tugged the flap shut and stepped away from him. As she cruelly jerked on his leash, I promised myself that next time I would carry some sort of dog biscuit to distract him, so as to avoid becoming complicit in her unthinking callousness.

After I escaped the elevator and any further social interaction, I managed to make it to my couch before collapsing and letting my exhaustion slough off me. Cadmium, my orange tabby who usually pestered me for food as soon as I walked in the door, sensed my inability to do anything more than slouch and resigned himself to perching himself on top of the couch. I sighed as I reflected on my day. I had had a detailed list of things to accomplish—all related to the death of my mother—and I had accomplished nothing but unearthing this symbol-made-flesh as I had let nostalgia overcome me just because some whim had coaxed me to wander past what had been our old breakfast spot.

I rubbed my eyes, thankful that they were organic, not metal. The trip, curtailed though it had been, had exhausted me. I dared not even begin to think of trawling through the job postings on the net to find a new contract. My last had ended a week before my mother had gone. In a moment of drunken and grieving desperation, I had even allowed my recruiter to put my contract out on the web to be snatched by any corporation willing to take a risk (and potentially a discount). I normally insisted on more control of my labor, but I couldn't find the energy to rouse myself from the fog of my grief. Or wine.

Despite it all, because of it all, I could not quite manage to figure out how to let go of my workpack. I kept it nestled in my arms as I dreamt.

Hours later, I stumbled awake to my door chime singing at me and Cadmium rushing at the door with his tail held enthusiastically aloft. Petra, I thought to myself. I'd given her my door code when she'd helped me with the flowers and the details and the overwhelming washes of sadness after the funeral.

I rearranged the workpack so that it lay within the crevice of my couch's pillows and sat up so that I could attempt to maintain some level of dignity.

Truly, though, there was never a need for dignity when Petra was around. My memories of her—by no coincidence—sang with the same bright, intense pitch as a rainbow. I say "no coincidence" because Petra's most obvious implants were strips of RGB lighting that raced around her arms and her fingers. She told everyone that she had had them done because the ambient lighting from them increased the efficiency of her coding and helped her to settle into her flow (she preferred a dim room alive only with soft music and soft fragrances, she claimed). I secretly believed that the unusual nature of the implants helped her branding for her gaming review side hustle.

This evening, the plastic of the takeout bags and the glass bottle of wine that she carried caught the rainbow light of her arms. Her smile was gentler than her lights would suggest; she had always been the staid, responsible friend, not the whimsical-as-a-skirling-leaf one. She would have been able to organize all the details of her mother's funeral so that her arm never ended up in a cybernetic recycling heap. I pushed aside my grimace at the mental aside so that I could return her smile when she said, "Vallaria, I thought you probably needed a night in. Hope you don't mind?"

Cardamom, cumin, garlic. The solidly grounding turmeric. The brightness of lemon. The prick of pepper. The stinging homeyness of my favorite takeout joint. We had shared so many of life's joys and tragedies over shawarma and lentil soup.

"How could I mind?" I asked. The swarming sadness that had been buzzing about my head abated. "This is just what I needed."

The conversation that night was a healing one. True friends know how to navigate the waters of grieving. They note the constellations of sorrow that sparkle in our eyes and do not press forward when the stars grow dark. They regale us with tales and sea shanties to help us forget the emptiness of sound when the wind no longer blows as it should.

There is no map for grieving, but our friends are our cartographers that allow us to find our way back to ourselves, nonetheless.

Petra did not talk about my mother or the fights I had had with my siblings. She did not ask about work or money or the responsibilities I had been shirking. Through her conversation she showed me that I could return to normal talk of relationships gone hilariously awry or books to be read; when she offered me a piece of baklava, she showed me that there could be sweetness in life to savor once again.

As we were reminiscing about our intro to philosophy class and how Petra had always threatened to write an essay rating the attractiveness of different philosophers, Cadmium begged for our scraps. As I shooed him away from me and toward Petra, my tablet beeped from within my workpack. With a muttered, "Just a minute," I tipped my pack onto its side to dig out the tablet, not having a sure enough hold on sobriety to pay attention to what might spill out. Petra struggled up from her cattywampus position on the floor and propped herself up on one of the throw pillows that I had thrown at her from the couch.

"What is that?" Petra asked, her tone oddly harsh. Petra seldom simply asked a question—she would circle around the back of whatever had aroused her curiosity and sweetly stalked it like prey.

I blinked as I looked at the screen. Blinked multiple times. The carnival lights that had overlaid the evening so far had dimmed. Disappeared. A dreary smear of gray was what remained. "It looks like EarthCar snatched up my contract." I tried to sit up straighter, but I felt my workpack tumble as I did so.

"EarthCar? Isn't that where your mom lost her arm?" I watched as her face lost saturation in real time. She was no longer focused on me but had let her glance slide past me.

"Yeah. I think I have a commendation they sent her sometime after the strike. It's buried in the office somewhere." My heart felt like all the coolant had dropped out of it. I sought to put a stopper in my emotions so that they didn't leak out all around me like a rusted-through radiator. "Petra, I don't know what to do . . . "

Still her gaze skipped over me like a startled needle on a record track. I followed her eyeline and saw what she had been staring at.

My mother's arm, loose on my couch, its lily-of-valley prominent and telling. Balanced in some sort of horrible symmetry with the job contract that lay beeping in my lap. It felt as though the implant in my head had restarted, short-circuited, been hacked by some cybernetically-enhanced hand of Fate. Everything slid into black and white and gray before my eyes like some strange facsimile of an ancient film reel. I closed my eyes briefly and rubbed them, hoping that the action would console me. It did not.

I instead grabbed my mother's arm and pulled it to my chest. "Oh Petra, won't anyone tell me what to do?"

"You should apply to art schools, Val."

I turned around. My mother had entered the room without my noticing. I'd been hiding my college brochures as best I could—I didn't want my siblings to mock me, and I didn't want to see the disappointment on my mother's face when she realized how much college would cost.

Besides, I hadn't won the art show at school. Hadn't even placed. Not after I had withdrawn my piece at the last minute because some asinine bully whose name I would never remember had asked if we even had enough money for paint at my house.

"My stuff's not that good, Mom. Besides, the best way to get out of here is to get into med school. Remember Tenney from two blocks down? That's what they did, and they're living downtown now."

"But I think your drawings are beautiful, Val."

Shame mixed with anger and roiled in my gut. I bit back all the poisonous words that others had thrown at me. My mother, the warehouse worker, wouldn't know Manet from Monet. Wouldn't know Basquiat from a basket. Would ask Yayoi Kusama if she bought her room decorations from the local multi-mart.

"Mom, what would you know? I won't even be able to go to college anyway. This is all just a stupid waste of time!" I swept the brochures off my bed and hurried out of the room lest she see the tears in my eyes.

"I know that I will always be proud of you," she said quietly, her heart torn out by my hurt.

In that moment, I wished so fervently that she would extend that metallic arm of hers and hold me close. Despite all the mockery I had endured for how outdated its technology was, how gauche it appeared, how pathetic I was that I had a mother with an arm meant only for doing labor (not anything beautiful or useful or intellectual), I longed to clamber into its embrace. Hers.

I never told her how I cherished her words in that moment. Not as I worked my way to my first real commission. Not when I received my first extended contract.

I had been too afraid to test her love for me aloud.

I told myself in the days after my mourning session with Petra that I hadn't made any decision. I couldn't.

It had been made for me.

Society is built too tightly, too constrictingly, to allow human beings to make moral choices. It smothers us as it layers responsibilities and contradictions upon us, its trowel smoothing over any imperfections in the mortar that weighs us down and aligns us in some uncaring scheme.

None of the other contracts that I had seen in the last three years paid nearly as much as EarthCar was offering; besides, I told myself, I would have had to pay a lawyer to get out of the contract since they had bought it outright from my recruiting agency. My mother's funeral had cost money that my siblings claimed not to have. My rent cost more money than I cared to think about.

Cadmium needed to eat. Often.

And I? I needed work to move me past my pain.

How can you make a choice when there is no choice at all?

I buried my mother's arm in my seldom-used hall closet. A few days after I did so, I guiltily abandoned a box full of never-used gardening implements in front of it.

That was that.

I spent the beginnings and ends of my workdays clamoring for a seat on the train; this one, however, led deeper into downtown instead of seeping toward the Verd. I spent my commute time counting the specters in the train car and allowing myself to forget that I, too, was merely haunting my own life. The breadth of the workday I spent scrounging for a desk in our office building, always hoping I would be able to find one next to a window so that I could do my design work while I watched the city below being glazed in the sticky sludge of the honey-colored light of the winter sun.

Like me, it seemed to struggle to complete its assigned journey every day. It barely managed to clamber above the horizon, and I dug into the moments it spent alight digging my fingers into the little warmth and joy it brought with it.

The work itself was good, though. Meaningful work that I was competent in. I and a small team were refreshing, reinvigorating the public face of EarthCar. I had done this sort of work before for smaller clients, so I felt comfortable in the work and comfortable in stretching my abilities to meet the needs of the new project. I had the money to order my round of drinks after work and to treat Petra to a weekend away when she and her partner broke up.

I never stepped onto a warehouse floor. I never feared the shrieks of metals or the blinding firefly sparks of a weld. I did not stand guard against the inevitable sound of a safety alarm being slapped off.

It was like working through a pleasant dream that was too nebulous and indistinct to hold onto upon waking.

However, I spent most of my weekends wandering through the urban clutter of the Verd. I imagined myself Theseus wandering through the Labyrinth, but with no Ariadne and no Minotaur. Nothing howled at me from some unseen center, and no one guided me forward.

I merely walked the streets, letting myself become lost in searching for something to search for. I let my gaze wander over the broken landscape of weather-beaten roadways and rust-encrusted metal structures, wallowing in whatever chromatic overlay my implant chose. I sought for something—perhaps meaning, perhaps inspiration for some new artistic endeavor that lay outside my routine workday. A route outside the rote. Whether the implant lay a rain-slick sheen or some industrial, molting patina before me, I found nothing in it.

So, I continued to spend my weekends walking, with no real beginning or end in sight.

It was three months into my EarthCar contract that the meandering path of my wandering straightened, became purposeful. The snow that piled in the streets, that blocked the storm drains and trickled through cheap boot soles to cold and tired feet, had picked up the grit of the Verd. No pure white here. Crevices and lumps of melted-and-refrozen snow were outlined in the gray grime of the pavement being scraped up by the occasional swipes of the snowplows. That sickly iridescence of a car's leaking oil caught the occasional weak ray of light. Of the yellow holes in the snow, the less said the better. But my implant captured it all, rendered it into some sort of obscure data.

As I crunched through the snow and felt my boots get heavier as they got wetter (resulting in my thoughts growing increasingly weighty as well), a familiar voice broke through the crust of my reverie.

"Hey Val! Baby Val! Is that you?"

I looked up. Somehow, I had ended up in front of my mother's best friend's home. Talia. *Her* mother had babysat my siblings and me when we were too young to be trusted not to murder or maim each other in the ramshackle rooms of our apartment alone.

I smiled as I was meant to. "Hey, Auntie T. It's been a while."

The part of me that became consumed by the idea of getting my Nimi implant when I was younger is the same part of me that wishes to say that when Auntie T invited me in, she gave me a homey, nostalgic fete. That her cooking awakened something in me, brought shivers of childhood memories to mind as my taste buds tingled.

It was not to be. Auntie T never could cook; she had refused to learn from her mother, whose recipes circulated much of the Verd. Auntie T preferred the carbonated rush of soda to the drinks that vids taught us that we should expect as guests; she never made any apologies for the popping of soda tabs being the harbinger of hospitality in her home rather than the whistling of a tea kettle or the bustle of a brewing pot of coffee.

She offered to reheat me a pork bun from the convenience store around the corner; of course, I had to accept. I sat in the chair at her kitchen table that had always been mine. I noted that she had finally fixed the chair spindle that I had kicked—then splintered—then cried about when I was almost a teenager.

As she brought the pork bun over to the table, she smiled and her usually wisecracking face glimmered. "You used to love these when you were small. You'd beg Momma to let you have some loose change so you could go sneak off and get one." She shook her head, but the smile clung to her face. "I bet you don't even remember that, do you?"

With a sinking of my gut, I realized I didn't. "I must have been really small," I said, trying to chuckle and save myself from embarrassment and a lengthy expiation of my sins, of not remembering.

"You were," she said. She looked as though she wanted to say something, but she choked it back. Were there tears in her eyes? I could not remember ever seeing that tell-tale glint in them before. Not unless she was laughing as we kids were making up some flamboyantly ridiculous childhood game or telling us a joke that our mother really wished she wouldn't. She reapproached the conversation. "What are you doing down here, anyway? Isn't your place up closer to downtown?"

Ah, the telling and retelling of sins that I thought I had avoided was about to begin. Auntie T wouldn't dance around a subject out of sympathy like Petra would. The long-formed habit of telling Auntie T the small pieces and ragged ends of something so that she could patch it all together into a quilted bit of truth was difficult to unravel myself from.

"Auntie, I don't really know. I just hopped on the train and started walking around. So much has changed."

"Yeah, you would think that there wasn't enough money down here for things to keep changing, but somehow, the streets keep shifting and the old places keep disappearing." She paused for a moment, then went off to grab a can of soda. After she had fidgeted with the tab enough for it to snap off in her hand, she said, "I heard that your old apartment building is getting pulled down in a month or two. Gotta make way for some more self-storage buildings, I guess."

"Maybe I should go check it out one last time before they tear it down," I said.

"I'm glad your mom doesn't have to see it," Auntie T said.

"Me, too." I took a bite of my meat bun. It had already started to cool, and the taste was nothing extraordinary, but the meat had begun to congeal in my mouth in a familiar, oddly comforting way. "I almost feel like if I wander around down here a bit more, maybe I'll run into her, you know?"

I hadn't known it was true until I said it, but once the words left my mouth, my weekends of solitary wandering suddenly had a retroactive purpose. It warmed me to realize that by saying it aloud I had bestowed meaning on all of those days of restlessness. I could feel the colors of Auntie T's kitchen warming at the edges of my vision. "Me too, kiddo," she said.

I realized that we had come to a ragged edge in our conversation—in our relationship, really. I had known her as a child, as a teenager. I wasn't fully comfortable in relating to her as an adult. I could feel that Auntie T felt the same way. "So, Val, I didn't have much of a chance to talk to you at the funeral. How's life been treating you these days?"

An innocent question, but when I tried to formulate a safe answer, my vision blurred.

Auntie T had worked beside my mother on the line at EarthCar for decades. As far as I knew, she still worked there. She had held her head up off the concrete floor when she collapsed after the accident; she had bandaged her head when a scab had pushed Mom into a barricade during the strike afterward.

The exits were where they had always been, but dread kept my feet locked to the floor. I looked at my hands, not at my Auntie. They shimmered, rainbow-sick and oil-slicked, as my guilty conscience unburied images and memories and emotions that I had preferred interred. "EarthCar bought out my contract, Auntie T." The next words tumbled out of my mouth quickly, in an attempt to outrun the shame I felt. "There was nothing I could do."

"What the hell, Val? You're working for them?"

My implant must have malfunctioned; some code compiled incorrectly, some zero had mistaken itself for a one. A circuit had flashed when it should have dimmed. All I knew was that I suddenly felt removed from everything I saw—touched, heard, smelled—and I watched Auntie T's face shatter like a carelessly dropped plate from afar. Like watching an old film, slowed down, played in reverse. I felt my hands tremble, but I dared not look at them. I dared not *perceive* them.

"Val, after all your mother went through? All you kids went through? You're working for them? Didn't your mom tell you that the docs think it was some chemical leaking in that bronze arm of hers that gave her the leukemia? That's why they amputated it when she died. They had to remove it to make sure they got rid of all the dangerous chemicals before they recycled it. They decontaminated it like they decommissioned her." She gathered her anger, and I watched it build as she launched into the next stage of her list of grievances, her grief. "EarthCar knew that model was obsolete when they forced it on her. Hell, girl, they knew it was dangerous! She died because they wanted to save a few bucks after their damned machines malfunctioned and cut her life in half in the first place! And now you're working *for* them?"

Breathing became difficult; I felt like I was sucking at the air like a drugged-up hummingbird sipping brokenly at a bird feeder. The cold came at me in waves, traveling up each individual nerve, threatening to drown me in the depths of my cold, cold thoughts.

I shook like I had as I left my mother's funeral.

"Oh Mother Above, Val. Oh, girl, I'm so sorry." Her eyes widened; her anger had blinded her. "I lost myself there. I'm just so *angry* at them. That's not the sort of thing you say to family." I felt Auntie T's arms, both warm flesh, wrap around me. My breathing calmed, and I pushed aside the jitteriness that had been skipping up my spine.

"It's ok, Auntie T. But she didn't tell me. I didn't know." Her arms held me tighter as I started crying.

Unbelievably, she laughed. Sharp, brittle, and sudden, and it broke as soon as it hit the air, but it was a laugh. "Of course she didn't. Your momma was a stubborn one." She stepped back from me and patted me on the head like she had when Cedar stole and dismembered my stuffed rabbit. She sat back in her chair, her posture more relaxed than it had been.

"I'm all fired up, I think. You might not have heard about it uptown in downtown, Val, but things are brewing down here. Down at the warehouses, down in the factories. Your momma's death was the final straw. There's talk of another strike coming. A bigger one, this time."

A study in incongruities, Auntie T. She had a smile on her face as words that should have been painful spilled out of her. "I hope you were proud of her, kiddo. She was our leader during the worst times. And as proud of her as we were, she was even more proud of you. She wore that lily-of-the-valley on her arm like a badge of pride. She could have buffed it out, but I don't think the thought ever crossed her mind."

She patted my hand. "That flower became our symbol, you know, during the first strike. A way of helping us remember that we had the love of people at home to keep us strong."

As I left her house, my limbs weak and my heart sore, everything around me took on a strange new hue. Something like spring sun passing through an almost translucent white flower. Something soft, something bright. Something that was more texture than light.

I had enjoyed the strange oscillations of color as my implant attempted to sync itself with the resplendent mess of hue that was the pieces of stained glass when Petra and I attended our first two stained glass classes. Over the years, I thought I had mastered the art of letting my consciousness float lightly atop the shifting tides of colors that my implant stirred; I had felt at home as the small ripples of visual change had uncoiled and spread across my perception, my sense of self. I had found a sort of joy in feeling my sense of self shift alongside the colors my implant brought me.

But not tonight. Not after that conversation.

I yearned for that sensation I had felt as I left Auntie T.'s. Light made material. Light suffusing the buttery dough meant for a holiday pastry as it was held aloft, stretched to transparency. Light passing through a rain-saturated canvas tent, weak and beautiful as it permeated the morning. Light with a texture, with a constancy.

Simpler, that. Closer to true. Less exhausting than this implant-mandated emotional tumult.

As I sat in the studio pretending a normalcy I did not feel, the wildly swinging colors were making me nauseous. As the Nimi implant sought the perfect, most beautiful shade for each, I felt like I was being tossed in a storm's waves. Or, more likely, caught in a riptide that was set upon drowning me in my own guilt.

I almost wished that I had cancelled. Petra would have understood. She understood everything.

I picked up a piece of tawny—ochre—golden—Naples yellow glass, ready to fit it into the larger whole. The Beatification of Saint Haraway, Petra and I had dubbed it. Patron saint of implants and cyborgs and women who sought trouble by creating and re-creating themselves. Top of Petra's list of now gone but always remembered philosophers.

As the lights changed and my consciousness wobbled, my hand slipped, and I sliced open my thumb. The piece of glass fell to the floor and broke. Without thinking I swept my injured arm and knocked a slew of other glass pieces to the floor as well, transforming those pieces into nothing but shards. The resulting noise matched its frequency to that of my panicked brain.

"Oh, Val! What happened?" Petra looked over, and upon seeing the bright ribbon of carmine where only yellow was supposed to thread, began rustling through her things for her first-aid kit. Of course she had one.

"My hand slipped. It must have been a long day at work."

Her eyebrow raised in anger but softened into worry. "You didn't work today. It's the weekend. You don't work weekends."

After she had wrapped my thumb and coaxed me into calm, she spoke to the instructor who reassured us that we could continue from where we left off in our next session. Petra wouldn't take no for an answer when she invited me out to grab some pie at a nearby dessert bar.

When we arrived, she grabbed us a table and then ordered a slice for each of us. I watched the rainbow lights of her RGB implants dance as we waited for our pie and our drinks. A waltz? I wondered. Ballroom? Twentieth-century break dancing? Funny, how the pattern of rainbow lights calmed me rather than exacerbating the vertigo I had felt in the stained-glass studio, despite their constant movement.

When the drinks arrived—one lavender-hued cocktail and one cup of warmly fragrant tea—I reached for the cocktail glass only to be met with a "Nope." Petra pushed the teacup gently in my direction. It was only when the pie slices arrived—hers a fruity explosion and mine redolent of cardamom and vanilla—that she said, "So."

I pushed my fork through my pie slice. Sweet and creamy, until the resistance of the pie crust. An apt metaphor, I thought, for how this conversation was going to go. But, in the moment I wasn't able to concentrate on the explanations I would need to make. All I could hold fixed in my mind were the taste of the pie and the rainbowed lights of Petra's fingers. "You never told me about your implants," I said.

Someone else might have mistaken my discursive attempt at conversation for an attempt at evasion. Petra knew me better, however; she was long accustomed to my discursive and recursive ways. "Odd that it never came up. Maybe because you had just been fired from that museum gig at the time? The one you thought was your dream job."

I sipped my tea. Cardamom there, too, nested among the other steeped spices. "I guess you did get them installed about then. What, four years ago? Five?"

"Not long after Sage was born." Sage, her sister's child. There had been some difficulty with the birth, I remembered. Petra had spent a month at her sister's place, helping out. She never really talked about that time, I realized. Nor did she discuss the specifics of her family often.

With a jolt, I wondered—how often did she not tell me things because I was too unsteady under the weight of my burdens?

She had kept talking, I realized. The stream of her narrative, the serenity of her voice, had swept past me as I basked in my guilt. More guilt added on top, then, as she said, "I realized that I wanted to make learning ASL special for us. Sage loves rainbows, so I decided to get the implants. The place I got them done had never done anything like this before." A brutal, short laugh, then, laced with rue. "Apparently afterward they used images of me for advertising, and it's become quite a thing in certain circles. Niche music and clubbing ones especially, I heard."

She paused to have some of her drink. "I bet Sage loves when you talk to them with your implants going," I said in order to bring back the happier Petra I knew.

"They do. I never knew before that implants could be a celebration like this. An act of love. I didn't realize how much emotional weight an object could bear." Petra's face lit up with a warmth that I could only imagine reflected the warmth on Sage's face when they talked.

She said, "You get it. I know you do. When I saw your mother's arm in your apartment, I was a little startled, but then I realized that you felt the same way I do." I busied myself with my pie then and concentrated on its homey taste so that I could block out the violently shifting colors my implant was picking up from the conversation and the flashing signs outside the bar. The streetlights, the headlights.

"Is that what tonight was about? Not knowing how to cope with working at EarthCar since they did so much damage to your mom? Val, you'll be ok." She reached across the table and held my hand for a moment. I liked the way the rainbows fell upon my skin but felt ashamed that I hadn't known their meaning for so long. I looked aside. Outside. She followed my gaze and caught our reflections in the bar window. "I love you for who you are, you know. You just get mired in all the ramifications of the decisions you make. It's like looking in this window here. You get a bit trapped in the reflections of all those problems—all these mirrors—that line your life. But you'll get there. You'll make your choice. You might just take a bit longer than some would."

She allowed the conversation to flow differently after that. The nausea passed as Petra infused the night with friendship and understanding.

I did not let her know that her kindness—and her loving assumption that I deserved her praise–cut me much more deeply than the glass had earlier.

I hoped for Petra's rainbow lights or the gentle-textured white light of my conversation with Auntie T, when I closed my eyes for sleep that night. Instead, a nightmarish kaleidoscope formed behind my eyelids. A memory, fractured and repeated and repeatedly fractured: my mother coming home after a day on the picket line, tired but (today) not newly bruised. I, confused, angry, and scared, picking a fight with her. As the kaleidoscope turned and the memories kept tumbling and falling, the next was a fight about having to fix dinner again. Another twist, another fumble, and this time I said something spiteful that mirrored the mockery the kids at school threw at me because of the strike. Another set of cruelly contrasting colors, and another iteration—my anger that she had ignored—had not sufficiently praised—a piece of artwork I had made for her—just for her!—and the hurt from which that anger had sprung. All those images, over and over. All those fragments.

When I woke up the next morning, I unearthed my mother's arm from my closet before I even asked the coffee pot to start brewing. Once I held it in my hands again, I did not quite know what to do with it. It seemed unnatural among my paints and things; it was not at home in the kitchen. I finally placed it on the coffee table in the living room, where it rested uneasily.

But the room took on its bronze sheen when I caught it in my peripheral vision.

I made eye contact with every ghost when I rode the to work. I looked my own reflection in the eyes and dared it to blink.

The difference in me built over a week, two weeks. The color of my coworkers' regard had begun to shift—but not in an unpleasant way. I had been known for my delicate approach to my work; reverent with images, arranging them like an old flower-shop pro perfectly placing focal flowers in bouquets. Now, I wanted to smash all my work and rearrange it with bloodied hands. I felt their admiration harmonizing with my building anger.

One email gave me the excuse to topple the rage I had been so wantonly assembling.

Someone in Marketing wanted to use the intersection of my mother's work experience with mine. I glowered when I read the email asking for a bio to put up on the website. I knew they were going to spin my history, then, to put the company in a pleasant light. My entire life would be scrubbed of the pockmarks of hardships that had roughened it, and my mother and I would become examples of how EarthCar supported families and was proud of its generations of tradition and whatever nonsense drivel came to the marketing intern's mind.

I knew why they snatched my contract, then.

My response, mere lines of text, eviscerated.

"Wow, Vallaria really went for the jugular on that one," my teammate Khanh said in a stage whisper. I basked in the stage lighting.

I heard her partner Maya whisper back, "All I can hear from Marketing is the gurgling."

Although I was pleased, I decided it would be a smart political choice to ask my manager for additional bereavement time.

When I arrived home that evening, I knew I had a week ahead of me. A week to let myself be cuddled by Cadmium. A week to sort through the mail and packages that had been sitting on my kitchen table. A week where I could finally work on Petra's birthday present. A week to till the soil of my creativity so that I could foster the growth of something I could be proud of again. A week to find out, really, who I was, who I had been, and who I was meant to be.

And a week to find out what to do with my mother's arm that lay so unceremoniously, so artlessly on my coffee table.

It is the paradox of the human condition that despite having hopes of creating so much meaning in my free time that I instead immediately sat on the couch and started mindlessly scrolling through videos. There had been a time in my education and early career during which

I couldn't watch these sorts of things without trying to analyze their construction and the semiotic tricks of the trade, but that part of my mind had fallen asleep long ago. After watching my third alpaca attack video, I stood and stretched and walked over to the kitchen. As I waited for my leftover Pad Thai to reheat, I sorted the important-looking mail on the table from the mailers and scams. Under a brochure for an interior decorator's services, I found a manila envelope. It was stiff and heavy with meaning. The sender's address? Auntie T's.

On a whim, I sliced open the envelope with my paring knife rather than opening it more carefully and conventionally. Inside was a short letter from Auntie T and a photographic still. I forced myself to read the letter from Auntie T first as a riot of colors screamed and crowded in from the edges of my vision.

Hey Val,

Sorry about the other day. I know things must have been rough for you lately, and I took everything I have been dealing with out on you.

We're family. We don't do that. I wanted to make it up to you.

So, I went and found this photo your mom printed of you. We were going to make you a collage for your birthday, I think, but we both forgot about it after the cancer diagnosis. I told her that these sorts of things were old-fashioned and that you would be embarrassed by it, but I think maybe I was wrong about that.

This was her favorite still of you. She used to take you to Green River Gardens for your birthday. Do you remember? When you were young, you'd have a birthday picnic there with her under the willow tree, tucked in with all the lilies-of-the-valley.

She was proud of you, Val. I think she'd even be proud of your new gig, believe it or not. Never saw her happier than when she got to talking about some new project you were working on. I think she knew every line of that flower of yours from memory.

Love,

Auntie T

I traced the "love" at the closing. None of us had ever been very open with our emotions. Not love, not anger (not after my teenage years), not pride.

I ignored the microwave as it beeped at me. I carefully took the edges of the photo and flipped it over, worried that my fingers would somehow smudge it, taint it.

It wasn't a photo of me. It was a photo of both of us.

The details of the photo began to fade before my eyes. I wiped my eyes with the back of my hand, but it came away dry. As I looked at the photo again, I realized that the details weren't fading; they were being swept away in a current of silky, golden light. Light the uplifting haze of summer would have envied. It was beautiful, it was yearning, it was love.

But it wasn't true. I put the photograph down on the table and immediately began a search on my tablet for how to disable my Nimi implant. A dozen truncated, forking paths later, I found what I needed. I quickly skimmed the list of possible side effects, but I decided nausea was an acceptable prelude to accepting a reality skinned of its aesthetic lies and pleasures.

When I finished the procedure, I looked at my photo again. Our photo. Though the memory wasn't perfect—I fear it was tattered at the edges—it was mine.

The fragrances of the day came back first. Fern crushed underfoot. The sugary brightness of a messily frosted cake, baked for just the two of us. The crisp cleanness of the Garden's air, trilled upon daintily by the serenading sweetness of a chorus of lilies-of-the-valley.

Then, I remembered her voice. There would never be any image or color or poetry that would describe the safety of it, the consistency of it—it was simply hers. I could hear her singing me a happy birthday, her voice vanishingly sweet.

Like Auntie T had written, we had come here every year for my birthday. She'd made sure that each of us had a special day dedicated just to ourselves. This one, the one in the still, was the last one. The last before she lost her arm, the last before I'd claimed that I wanted to spend the day at an arcade with my friends. But I remembered it well, though I had not known at the time that it would be the last time in my life she alone would sing just for me.

As she served me a second slice of cake ("every day and every life should have a second chance at sweetness," she had said), she looked around the garden. The light caught her cheekbones, and in that moment, she was my ideal made living flesh. "Vallaria, did you know that I named you after these flowers?"

"My name's not Lily, Mom!"

She laughed. "Your name is short for *Convallaria majalis*. That's the scientific name for lilies-of-the-valley. I didn't think you'd appreciate *that* name as you grew older. I didn't think Connie would fit you quite right, either. But, my little Val, this is the place—this spot right here—that you are named after all the same."

I drank in her words. These moments of truth are more potent than any wine. There is nothing more intoxicating than hearing the story of your life—the story of your very being—narrated by one who loves you.

"When I was pregnant with you, I visited here and sat among these flowers. Lilies-of-the-valley. I know that they are beautiful and pleasant and fragrant, but look at how strong they are!" Here, she flicked at one of the stems. The bell-blossoms trembled, but not with fear or the possibility of falling. They trembled like a triangle in an orchestra.

"They seem so fragile, but so much beauty depends on such delicate stalks. They bend, but they do not break." She blew upon the stem, then, but there was no soft explosion like there would have been with a dandelion. "They dance upon the wind, but they remain whole. Their curving delicate forms are their strength. That was my first birthday wish for you, Vallaria. That you would be strong enough not to break, even when you must bend. And, artist that you are," (here I blushed that she was saying my secret dream aloud), "I have the feeling that much beauty will come from you, too."

I squirmed with happiness then and told myself that I would never forget that day. I had, of course. I had made hundreds of promises to my mother, and I had broken most. But looking at that photograph and seeing for the first time how closely my smile mirrored my mother's own, I knew I could change.

But now, I promised myself, I would remember. Forever.

I looked out into the living room, where my mother's arm still lay. My earlier preoccupation with where it lay seemed silly now. Childish. Where I put it had nothing to do with respecting her or honoring her memory. It was what I did with it that was important. I took my paring knife to hand and gently—so gently!—I reinscribed each line of the lily-of-the-valley on my mother's arm. Each stroke was an act of rebellion against the me I had used to be; each scratch upon the bronze flesh of her arm was an act of love.

I was rebuilding my memory of my mother—my love for her—with each line of the flower that I invoked again on the surface of her arm.

As each line flowed fluidly down my paring knife, as fluidly as ink from an antique pen, I realized a truth that had never before cleared the horizon of my thinking. Our physical acts become memory; our memories reside, abide, *live* in the space that our actions create. In our decisions, in our reactions, in every beat of movement we make, our memories reinscribe our natures upon ourselves. They breathe, and they are our breath.

And as I fell drowsily toward my dreams, I caught the scent of lilies-of-the-valley. It was as if they, too, breathed in my apartment.

I fell asleep that night, mentally sketching out the "old-fashioned" version of the photograph that I would paint for Auntie T. Watercolors, my old nemesis, seemed old-fashioned enough, I thought. I slept soundly enough that not a single dream crept past the threshold of my subconscious.

I awoke at first light. With Cadmium curled up upon my lap, I sent two messages. One to EarthCar, terminating my contract and damning the consequences. Financial pain was much easier to bear than the moral kind. The other I sent to Petra, telling her I *needed* to meet her for brunch. I had made my choice, I wrote to her. I could imagine her cloud-breaking grin when I told her that I was going to join the warehouse and factory workers. Perhaps Auntie T could help talk the union into letting me help them with their messaging and their graphic design, I would say.

The morning light was pure and true.

I could imagine it now: lilies-of-the-valley spreading everywhere that the workers marched. Strongly pushing past the inert cold of winter into the gentle strength of spring.

I would join them down at the warehouse; I would walk the line down at the factories. Auntie T *would* convince them of the worth of my words and the power of my images. They would find space for me, I knew.

I could help their voices rise. Sing.

My mother would be in the strength of my voice and in my willingness to let it ring with heartache. To be vulnerable like the trembling white blossoms of my childhood.

Together we would push past that which conspired to hold us down. We would be brave enough to bend but brazen enough to never break.

Though we might tremble in the winds of change our actions brought down upon us, we would carve our dreams—a new future—into being. Together.

ABOUT THE AUTHOR

Samara Auman is a speculative fiction writer who lives in the mossy Pacific Northwest with her husband and two appropriately mischievous cats. She believes the PNW to be one of the most delightfully uncanny places on the planet. Her work has previously appeared in *Clarkesworld*, as well as in venues like *Fireside Magazine* and *Diabolical Plots*.

The Blinding Light of Resurrection
RAJEEV PRASAD

Hands trembling, Shiv Mehta snatched the print copy of his wife's ribcage off the conveyor belt and lowered the print into an organ tank. Those hands had healed thousands of patients, but these days his hands had gotten good at stealing.

Over the last few months of his wife's treatments, he'd fought all the fights with his colleagues. Each week, the ethics committee had convened bright and early, while Penelope slept in a morphine haze. They'd convened over sweet, steaming coffee, while the cancer ate through her chest. The bastards had ultimately denied them access to more body prints, so, Shiv had resorted to drastic measures.

He rolled the suitcase towards the vestibule. *Sorter*, a six-foot tall robot shaped like a chrome beak processed the last remaining prints on the conveyor belt—a kidney and kneecap. Its aluminum pincer opened and closed like it was lifting a baby chick as it placed each organ into regenerative suspension for tomorrow's cases.

Shiv had helped create Sorter, so naturally he had full clearance to the print lab. He'd scrubbed his wife's antigenic signature from her print, creating a sort of immunogenic blind spot, to evade Sorter and prevent immediate disposal of her print.

He'd coupled a surveillance camera glitch to the nightly self-diagnostic program and the systems would be coming back online soon. He raced out of the lab towards his office.

The wheels of his suitcase thudded on the linoleum floor as he hurried to his office. The hour wasn't so late, about six pm, but the cases were scheduled and completed early at ReStart hospital.

Inside his office, Shiv slumped against the wall to stay upright. Once the nerves passed, he pulled off his scrubs. He scrunched his nose at his acrid odor—the smell of hard work—from having operated all day.

His gaunt, gray reflection and wild, unkempt silver hair amused him as he washed in his office shower and put on a fresh pair of scrubs.

For forty years, he'd kept the same office, adjacent to his operating suite that contained his robotic mimic—a rectangular quantum computer with a set of identical neo-skin hands.

Mounted on his office console were a pair of mesh gloves that sometimes reminded him of a knight's chainmail. He slipped his hands into the fine mesh. The micro-fabric tightened around the contours of his hands and buzzed as they synced with his nerves and muscles. He felt at ease, comforted. His mimic counterpart flexed its android hands from behind the window.

A loud knocking on his door startled him. His hands contorted in mid-flexion.

He deactivated his mimic and released the lock under his desk. The door opened and in ambled Harry Weinstock.

Age hadn't been as kind to Harry. Carrying too much weight, thinning gray hair, nose reddish and bulbous from too much wine. After they'd completed their training, they'd worked together to pioneer the field of body printing. Harry had been on the pathology and immunology side, whereas Shiv had orchestrated the biomechanical engineering and surgical process.

"I saw your office and mimic were still active. You're here late," Harry said.

"I could say the same for you. Need something?"

Harry nodded pensively. "Got a minute? There's been missing prints, and I can't figure it out for the life of me."

Shiv glanced at his suitcase but quickly recovered with a stony poker-face and shrug. "No clue."

"Any idea, any thoughts on how that could be happening?" Harry said.

"The print lab's always been your domain."

"It's the strangest thing, for months there's been a mismatch between the tissue generated and the actual prints."

"Can't help you." Shiv cleared his throat. "I should be getting home. Been another long day."

Harry's face creased up with a searching sidelong gaze. "I know it's been hard. I'm sorry."

"You would know best, wouldn't you?"

"Shiv!" Harry pleaded. "The whole committee agreed that we were prolonging Penelope's suffering."

Shiv stared at him, the malice growing. "Is there ever a good time to die, Harry?"

"She was my best friend. We were all hurting." Harry stood up, eyeing the suitcase. "You going somewhere?"

"It's easier to roll than carry a briefcase. I'm old, now." Shiv forced a chuckle.

"I'll give you a ride home, at least."

"The train works just fine, Harry."

"I'm sorry about, her. I really am. Anyway, we've got to make some changes to the print lab soon."

Shiv powered down the console and the office darkened. "What kind of changes?"

"Tighten up the process. Might be the right time for you to move onto the next phase."

"When we're ready, Harry."

They left the office and started in opposite directions down the long empty hallway. Harry called back over his shoulder, "*We?*"

The paint peeled off the cracked wood of Bly Manor like purple candy ribbons. Located just a block off the lake, nestled between a tree-lined street and forested park, the stately Victorian had once seen lavish parties, fundraisers, holiday gatherings, even Penelope's nieces wedding receptions. But now it was a lonely house damaged from storms two years back—a front gutter hanging off the roof and a particle board ramp over a broken porch step.

Shiv glanced over both shoulders as he approached the front door. Despite the house's dilapidated state, the neighbors still gave him wide berth and lenience. The sun had set early, by five, as it did in late November, and a biting wind blew off the lake.

Inside, white bedsheets covered the couches and teak wood table. Shiv opened the fridge and wolfed down a half-eaten tuna sandwich and drank his health supplement. He heard the shrill, desperate barking from downstairs. His face broke into a wide smile, his first genuine feeling of joy that day.

He reached the doorway to the basement level. The double doors slid open, and the old wood and aging beams gave way to a metal tunnel that ended in a vestibule. He basked in a sterilizing mist as a rapid test was performed for any pathogens that might still be in a prodromal or latent phase. Adjacent to the vestibule was his surgical chambers. He'd installed an exact copy of his mimic and quantum robotic surgeon. He'd sold their luxury cars. He'd sold their boat. He spent their fortunes on building this operating room to save her.

He passed through another set of double doors into Penelope's quarters. Willow whined and limped circles around him, until rolling onto his back and waiting for a belly rub. He was an old dog, near twenty now. He hobbled along gleefully. His hairless rump, a non-immunogenic pig print, stuck up beyond the height of his back.

Penelope reclined in her automated wheelchair staring into their backyard. Three blinking lights from video surveillance cameras periodically lit up the dark pines and barren winter maples. She turned to face him. Her right lower jaw was partially removed, and her sinus cavity remained exposed and covered with a clear protective coating. "I was going mad. Thank God your home." Her words echoed and distorted in a light whine though the sealed sinus chamber.

He knelt by her wheelchair. "I'm so sorry, but today I got the print."

"That's good news," she said without a smile.

"Are you ready for surgery? I don't think we should wait."

"I'm ready to get it over with."

He lifted her white gown and inspected the right side of her chest, nearly half still missing after the last remaining tumor removal a few weeks ago. Her heart gyrated rhythmically in the cavity. The embryonic lung was growing quickly.

"Your blood markers shows that the sarcoma is in *total* remission. Now we need to print out the two last remaining parts and make you whole."

"I'm a success!" She laughed wryly and rotated her chair to face him.

Her alabaster skin on the good side of her face was smooth and her eye and smile expressive. Her will to survive made his work feel organic and natural. His dedication to heal her kept him relevant.

"The strangest thing, I got an email from Harry an hour ago. A two-pager that he missed me. It was the most precious thing. He was always so sentimental."

Shiv nearly choked on his spit. "An hour ago?"

"So much feeling in just an email. I'd forgotten what it's like to have some passion. We're so focused on surviving."

"Don't forget it was Harry who did this to us. He's the one who stopped your care," Shiv said.

She rested her hand on his and squeezed affectionately. "I don't blame him for doing his job. I don't blame you for doing what you needed to do. But it's been hard. That's the truth of it."

"It's only until you're cured. We are so close," Shiv said.

"I want to believe that, but can I resuscitate my life. I don't know?"

"He was out of line sending that letter. We are so close now."

A mischievous smile formed on the good half of her face. "More than half of my body is printed. So, in a way you've been two-timing."

"Never!"

"It's truth. I'm a different woman." She winked.

"You're even more exceptional," Shiv said. "Of course, you didn't respond to him."

"I wanted to, but I know what's at stake. So, are you going to take me for an evening stroll on the balcony, before you cut me open, again?"

"Do you have to be so callous?"

"I'm the one going under the knife, Shiv. A little humor helps me endure."

He assisted her out of her chair. Her left hip print from a couple weeks ago had enmeshed beautifully. She was walking with just a slight limp.

"What I'd give to go for a jog again," she said.

Shiv cocked his head as he remembered what a fabulous runner she'd been. "I'd forgotten."

"Track and field could only take a girl so far."

"I'm forgetting so much about us," Shiv lamented.

"Because you're so obsessed with rebuilding my body, but it's just a body, Shiv. Eventually it will give out."

"Not anytime soon," he said.

Willow wobbled behind them on his hind pig legs, excited to get a chance to explore the scents and terrain of their terraced backyard. Penelope shivered in the cold, but she refused to go back inside. She treasured every chance to be outside and feel the connection to the natural world. Broken and battered, a collection of incisions and scars, she'd suffered day after day, month after month, but she was finally healing. Her chin tilted up and she consciously breathed in the cool night air like it was bringing her body back to life. She limped up and down the concrete steps, while their pig-dog barked at creaking branches.

Not all families were the same. Not all were healthy and adjusted. Not all aged gracefully without scars. Shiv was determined to ensure that this strange family of theirs still had a future together.

An hour later, Shiv sat in darkness while a white light bathed Penelope's clean skin. Her chest print floated in the organ tank's red-tinged nutrient suspension.

Inside the operating vault, the mimic rolled adjacent to Penelope's body and hovered above her. From behind the glass, Shiv flexed and twisted his hands, and the neo-skin hands of the mimic followed his precise movements. He calibrated each digit and thumb.

"Are you ready, love?"

She was already asleep as the sedative coursed through her body. The mimic hands lifted the print from the suspension. The dome of tiny cameras zoomed onto the surgical site and created a three-dimensional holographic view for Shiv.

He inspected Penelope's ribcage, the various pock-ridden ribs and wasted muscle. This part of her body was like a war zone of land mines, cracked concrete, and shattered glass. The mimic removed the damaged tissue, then identified the native vessels, nerve complexes, and lymphatics. The mimic hands probed and pushed as Shiv anastomosed the vital connections.

Penelope's face was calm and serene like the face of death. She was neither in the place of waking nor the place of dreams. She was under the knife, as close to death as a person could possibly be. And he was the one who was responsible for bringing her out of that dark well, back to their home, back to the world of the living.

At dawn, Shiv checked the surgical site, and the mimic ran measurements on tissue health and immune tolerance. She was barely awake, still under the influence of the sedatives and pain control. The rib cage was enmeshing slower than expected. The skin a shade darker than the rest of her body and the breast tissue was lopsided, but those cosmetic alterations would be an easy fix once she was healthy.

Shiv arrived at ReStart with time to spare but was surprised to find that he'd been reassigned from his morning case. The chief had assigned him to peer review. A couple years ago, an epic tantrum would have been in the works, and he would have scorched the chief and every one of his young surgeons, but not anymore.

What mattered now was making sure he developed Penelope's last print—the right side of her face.

He spent the morning signing off one case after another. Into his third cup of coffee, he saw a note from Harry asking him to meet him in the immuno-pathology department right next to the body printing chamber.

His heart raced and he knocked over his paper cup. The dark liquid ran over the edge of his table and pooled on the floor. He knew Harry suspected him. He also knew finding any evidence to use against him would prove elusive.

Shiv strolled into the surgical lounge. The heady, day-end banter came to an abrupt halt. He nodded politely to the other surgeons, OR techs, and nurses. A dozen flutes of sparkling apple and grape juice surrounded a spread of smoked fish and cheese and olives. The personal stories of the patients played on a wide screen. It was a good day-end tradition that he and Harry had started so many decades ago, but now he felt like an outsider here. This was a celebration of life. He had become myopic in his battle to stave off death.

When he'd been young and mid-career, the prestige, the fame, the money had still mattered. They had been his substitute for joy. Obsession was the steady cry of the void that had always been inside him. The sense of difference had started even in grade school. While the other boys had been playing ball and chasing girls, he'd been contemplating the fragility of the human body, the impermanence of identity. And Penelope had always accepted this dissonance about him. She was the lightness, the humor, the basis for their connection to others.

Without her, he was joyless.

He reached the immuno-pathology lab and Harry removed his hands from the robotic arms under the hood and pulled off his visor. "Thanks for coming, Shiv."

"Haven't been down here in a while."

"The glamour is all upstairs."

"Not for me. Zero cases today," Shiv said.

"My chance for glamour ended sometime around grandkids," Harry said.

Shiv's expression softened. "You see them much?"

"Almost never. I was a real lousy dad. Karma sucks." Harry looked down the row of work hoods and labs stations. "This was our lives, Shiv. The progress came at a cost."

"This was never a cost to me. This was my reward."

"You're built differently. Penelope always knew that about you."

At the mention of her name, Shiv's shoulders rolled back and stiffened. "So, what do you need?"

"I wanted to talk about the missing prints?"

"Come on, that's your paranoia. There's no way any print could get past Sorter."

Harry rubbed his left knee and wobbled like an arthritic penguin towards the sorting room. "Shiv, I know you hold what happened with Penelope against me, but the committee made a collective choice."

"It's old news, Harry."

"Not so old, just ten months. About the time when the missing prints started." Harry entered his code to Sorter's chamber. When Shiv didn't follow, he said, "You coming?"

They washed and gowned and stepped into the bright lights of the print chamber. Sorter's long metal beak hung downwards along its suspension pole, but as they entered the chamber, a series of blue lights lit up along its base and its beak swiveled upwards. Once it surveyed and cleared them, it returned to an inert position and the blue light shut off.

Shiv admired the creature's intelligence, the efficiency in keeping its domain clean of dangerous microbes and unwanted intruders.

Harry walked past Sorter and patted the steel wall. "The generator behind this wall takes days to produce the patient's nerve, bone, lymph, and all the elements needed to make flesh. The percentage of tissue produced deviates within acceptable limits to the actual mass of the prints. That number keeps hovering between one to two percent above the limits each month, but Sorter isn't detecting any missing or anomalous prints."

"I understand the process," Shiv said.

"We've never designed much surveillance into the printing process, since it's so specialized to each patient and case."

"It's likely an intrinsic generator error."

"The AI is under intense internal controls, so unlikely. But *you* have a reason to sabotage me."

"Harry, that is a terrible accusation!"

"It wasn't my fault that we couldn't do more for her. Dozens of prints. A year of surgery, radiation, and chemo. She was suffering, but you couldn't see it."

"Do not talk to me about *my* wife! She was my wife Harry, not yours. Remember that."

"Oh, I know. But we were close once. Closer than you realize."

Shiv's entire body clenched, and his head felt like it was buzzing. He seethed, "What are you saying?"

"I didn't want her to suffer, because I cared about her."

Shiv waited now, slowing his hyperventilation, realizing he was on the brink of a catastrophe. He kept his lips sealed to keep from slipping up and revealing too much.

Harry straightened out and sucked in his gut. "It's my guess that you have been doing something wonky in the print lab to get back at me and get me fired. You're the only one with the know-how to mess with the prints."

Shiv replied calmly, "Ask yourself why I would go through such heroics over *you*? I am not trying to get you fired or ruin your legacy. End of story. Check everything in my office and database. You'll find nothing."

"I want to believe you, but I don't," Harry said.

Shiv sighed. "Let's put this behind us and go to the deli for a sandwich."

"I'm suspending your privileges to the printer. You can go through the normal channels like the rest of the surgeons."

"Harry! You don't even have the authority to do that. Let alone a reason."

"I don't, but the board does. I'll be curious to see if there's any more missing prints after they make their decision in the next couple days."

Shiv nodded. Anything he said now could expose him. He glanced back at Sorter's inert body and was consumed with a sense of hopelessness. His legs trembled at the thought of leaving Penelope without half her face, without being able to make more prints should she need. He was cornered, but he wasn't about to give up, not when they were so close.

"Let's go." Harry stood behind the doorway peeling off his gown.

"On second thought, Harry, I don't want to go out to dinner."

The following night, Shiv stayed in his office into the quiet haunting hours. At one am, eyes bleary and heavy, he crept out into the hallway and snuck down the stairwell to the basement level. The skeleton janitorial crew was upstairs cleaning, so he was left alone.

He was comfortable in the underbelly of a hospital. It was his place of refuge, his place to daydream. His clear knowledge of muscle layers, tumors, bone, nerve, and lymph, of all things anatomical and physiological was his magic to brave the hellscape of illness. His mimics and his three-dimensional holo-wear were his talismans and artifacts.

He imagined himself lurking in purgatory itself, but death was not his enemy. Death was quiet. It did not speak from the void. But the wails, the crying of those who remained, were the sounds that haunted him. The sound of a father wailing in a waiting room. The wife who couldn't leave the side of her child's corpse. How he hated having failed those lovely people who had found love and intimacy in a way that he never could.

That he'd been sorely neglected as a child, that he'd been incapable of forming friendships, was irrelevant to him. That sad boy was gone. He was now Shiv Mehta with all the accolades and armor that came with his name. But most of all, he always would be Penelope's devoted husband.

He ran the self-diagnostic program to switch off the lab surveillance. He arrived at the print lab to find Sorter reclined in a hibernative reboot. His wife's print was there waiting at the edge of the conveyor. He'd managed to sneak it in before the board suspended his print privileges. He placed it into his briefcase and raced through the hallway with a feeling of immense joy.

Outside, he splashed through the puddles in the alley, only to find that the trains had stopped running. He was a specter now under the skyscrapers of the Chicago skyline. Each cubicle light reminded him of a scream into the dark night. He raced on towards the lake. The cold was biting, but he felt a rush, the thrill of success. Her print in his suitcase was climate preserved, being nourished, readying for its final mission to heal Penelope, to make her whole.

The Taxi brought him home about half an hour later. He entered the house like a thief. She and Willow were asleep downstairs, so he chose to sleep upstairs on the couch. And if he could have, he would have hugged the print to his chest like a stuffed teddy bear.

The following morning, after a rare cathartic sleep, Shiv woke well after sunrise. He brewed two cups of coffee and ventured downstairs. He washed and cleared disinfection and passed into their quarters, now flooded with morning light, Willow immediately began jumping on his leg.

"Penelope. Penelope?"

No answer. Willow barked wildly and gyrated on his pig legs and Shiv rubbed his ears gingerly. The Egyptian cotton bedsheets were neatly folded on her bed.

A shadow crossed over the hardwood flooring, and he glanced outside. She was standing in the sunlight. With just her cane, she'd walked out to the porch and now stood entirely exposed to the elements. He nearly shrieked.

He hurried to the porch and led her back inside. "Penelope what are you thinking? You know you have surgery today."

"I have surgeries every week, honey. Did you even notice how well I'm walking?"

"It's remarkable. Your hip has healed beautifully."

"Did you notice the glorious sunrise?"

Her chin was tilted up, exposing the web like stranding of the damaged side of her face. Her eyes possessed a surprising determination that he hadn't seen in a while.

"It's so strange but Harry has been sending me more notes."

"Has he? He's getting confused from all his boozing. Grasping for ghosts."

"I remember when I had to choose between you two. Back then it wasn't much of a choice. I adored you, what you stood for, how you changed into someone more vulnerable only around me. But Harry really did adore me."

Shiv cleared his throat and took a calming breath to get comfortable with this rather unexpected discussion. "Those early years with you were the happiest of my life. It was the first time I had ever felt anything. Until you, my life had been gray."

"I knew how much you wanted to accomplish, but I also knew you needed me to survive, to do what God intended for you to do.

"I'm so glad you did."

"We made a life together, but it wasn't easy for me. I had to sacrifice so much to make it work, so you could do so much good."

"It's your success as much as it is mine or Harry's. Without you, this all would never have happened. The thousands and thousands of people we've saved is because of you," he said.

"But the difference is I am hollow, and you are not."

Shiv wondered if he'd put her through too much. He knew that death was coming for all for them, but he'd engineered them more time. Time was all they had left, and with time came hardship and suffering but also tiny moments of happiness.

"You'll have another chance, soon."

"I want to read you Harry's note from today. It's not going to be easy for you to hear." She walked over to her computer and pulled up the screen.

Dear Pene, it's the strangest thing but lately I feel like you are still here. I spent a lot of time with you in the hospital and saw how much you were hurting. Please forgive me if I made the wrong choice. But the cancer was a real fucker, and we went with preserving your dignity. When I close my eyes, I remember a younger version of you with auburn hair and dimples. Your smile made me laugh, but also cry because you weren't mine. I cried because I couldn't see that smile every night and every morning. I loved you so badly that it hurt, for years, but I was just your fat little pathologist pining away in his lab. But I could have given you a good life, Pene. I could have. I miss you.

Shiv took a deep breath to quiet the hammering in his temples. "He's got some nerve."

She shrugged and strolled around her wheelchair. Her supple and relaxed movement was something Shiv hadn't seen in a long while. "It's like a journal entry, a confession. He doesn't think anybody is reading it."

"What a bastard," Shiv said.

"It's endearing. I think we're all past the choices of forty years ago."

"Apparently he's not."

"Memories are made to be replaced. We've lived a rich life, but his marriage was cold and short, and he divorced so young. He never created new memories with someone else to replace those old ones."

"Your generosity is amazing. You see the best in people."

"But now I'm seeing I missed out on things I needed to feel, maybe even do, to make my life fuller."

"I'm sorry, but you'll have time now," he said.

"Harry had an intuition, some sixth sense about me. Otherwise, why would he be writing me letters."

"Things are very tenuous right now."

"Tenuous how?"

"He's onto the missing prints. You need to be one hundred percent so we can escape somewhere and start new."

A knowing grin formed on the good side of her face. "He's had an intuition that I'm still here on this Earth."

"I hope this is the last print. I do."

"He was fighting for me too. He wanted to end my suffering. You wanted to give me a second chance. You both were doing the right thing in your own way."

"You told me you wanted to live. That's why I did this."

"I did." She nodded pensively. "I wanted to live because I knew you needed me to live. And I wanted you to go on with your life without regret, without always asking *what if*. That was a sacrifice that culminated in *this*."

She opened her arms and embraced the empty space between them like it held her derailed ambitions, her unrealized dreams, even the children that they'd never had.

He sighed with his gaze downcast. "So, what do you want me to do."

"What you always do. Finish the job."

He drank a focus tea and began his preparations for the print replacement. Penelope went through the motions of undressing, sterilizing, and reclining on the cold steel table, like a concubine waiting for her unwanted lover.

Once she'd been sedated and oxygenated, the ghostly mimic hands moved over his wife's inert body. He stared through the mirror and felt a strange anger and sadness twisting inside of him. He took a few deep breaths, calming his mind, but still the feeling persisted. He realized it was because of Harry and these letters.

He wondered if they'd had affairs over the past forty years. They'd always been so friendly, so comfortable around one another. For a moment he felt like retching at the thought of his lovely wife naked with that repulsive man. He couldn't shake the feeling. Why else would Harry be writing her love notes.

He noticed the mimics quivering above the table. If the robot had eyes, it would have been looking at him searchingly asking *what in God's name is the hold up?*

Shiv put on some instrumental rock from the turn of the century and listened carefully to the wailing electric guitar and the symphonic chords. He eased away the emotions like swatting away flies. Years of training were of course paramount in this sort of emotional repression. Once his mind was calm, he returned his attention to Penelope's neck and jaw. Right now, in the sleep of anesthetic death, Penelope needed him to do his job as a surgeon.

The holographic glasses descended over his eyes. The mimics removed the print from the nutrient-stem suspension and danced above her body to their own symphonic quantum music. The mimics proceeded delicately and slowly as they put her face back together. He intervened and corrected the mimics occasionally when he saw a slight mismatch in facia. The vessel stitches he did himself. The skin graft fit perfectly. All in the all the surgery was an astounding success.

But before he disconnected, the mimics alerted him to an unhealthy line of tissue along her ribcage. Shiv's eyes widened and he found himself holding his breath. The rib's entire anastomoses line was gray and dusky. He ordered a perfusion scan, and the mimic moved a green sensor over her pale skin. The three-dimensional images formed, and Shiv saw that the anastomoses to the native vessels hadn't taken. He realized that he hadn't been diligent enough in ensuring the native vessels were free of any adhesions from the scar tissue. Now it was too late. The ribcage tissue was dying and needed to be removed, which meant he needed a new print.

Shiv slept a few hours and arrived at ReStart around three am. He avoided the main halls and went straight to the basement to his console where he'd installed a scrubbing program. Fortunately, there was enough of Penelope's remaining tissue available, so he ordered the print with a hacked printing code that he'd used once in the past. Anything he did now would alert Harry, but he had no choice. He removed the antigenic signature from Sorter's recognition and planned to pick up the print in the next couple hours.

Shiv snuck back outside through the basement side doors venturing into an alley where thick steam hissed from the vents. Here he caught his breath. A feeling of helplessness permeated the milky air. He'd been helpless when they'd chosen to pull the metaphorical plug on her. He wouldn't let that happen again.

He strode in through the front entrance to his office to find Harry waiting inside.

"How did you get in here?"

"I've got a master key. It's a hospital's office. You just work here," Harry said.

"Are you a facility manager now? For forty fucking years, I've worked in this office, so it might as well be mine."

"It's not."

"What do you want, *Harry*?"

"Pissy this morning, *Shiv*?"

Shiv strolled inside and threw his briefcase onto his desk. The sprawling office felt cramped and tight like he couldn't get enough air. His palms were sweaty.

"Your privileges to the print lab are suspended as of this morning. I wanted to let you know in person."

Shiv shrugged as if it didn't matter. "I have nothing to do with your missing prints."

"Precautionary. Every print will need my direct entry. Period."

"I create and examine every print before surgery. I've done that for—"

"—forty years. Yes, I know Shiv, but times are different."

"Leave me out of your witch hunt."

"I've made my decision. It applies to *all* the surgeons." Harry strolled around the office inspecting some old photos, his gaze settling on one of Penelope. Almost like he was talking to himself, he said, "She was lovely."

A black fire engulfed Shiv's heart.

"I've been thinking about her a lot lately. How one single woman could have affected the two of us so deeply."

"Don't jump off that cliff," Shiv whispered.

"It's too late. Already jumped off it a long while ago."

"What are you saying?"

"There's nothing left to say." Harry waddled towards the door.

"What about my prints?" Shiv called out after him.

"No more prints, unless I enter them manually." Harry closed the door behind him.

Shiv was caught in a sort of dissonance. The calming, methodical nature of work, which to him was like putting one foot in front of another, was his bedrock, and he felt it cracking apart under his feet. He didn't remember much from his childhood, but a vague impression of his father occurred to him. His father, who'd worked as a mechanical engineer until the day he died, would often say that *A man spends most of his life alone. Work is the best way to be alone, to realize who you are and what this world intended you to be.*

Whether or not his father had intended, Shiv had lived his life in that way.

Until Penelope had gotten sick, he'd never understood how much she had meant to him. And she and Harry had betrayed him. That much was becoming clear in the primitive murk of his emotional understanding. How? When? The details? None of that mattered now. He held his face like it was a theatrical prop and wailed like a wolf. Then the crack started like a surgical incision rendering him open from head to toe, and from inside came the necrotic soul that had been denied joy for its entire life.

He raised his hands in front of his face, but they felt disembodied. His hands of resurrection were not his; they never had been. The deep power of his unconscious shadow had guided those hands.

He needed to finish his life's work. He was going to heal Penelope.

Which meant he needed to silence Harry for two reasons. First, he needed continued access to the print lab for at least this last print. Second, with Harry gone, Penelope would get over him, absolve herself of this stain over them.

Harry's old lab coat had been hanging on a door hook for a couple weeks. Shiv carefully brushed off the neck with a sharp blade and extracted two white hairs from the shoulder.

Into the immunologic sampler they went. The dead skin and hair gave him a precise antigen matching for his so-called friend. Oh, how Harry must have comforted and consoled her. Shiv seethed. Spit flew from his mouth and his eyes bulged. Harry fucking Weinstock.

Once the unique antigen matching was complete, he put on his coat and raced to the basement. He found his workstation and loaded Harry's precise sequencing into Sorter's program. Then, he ran his scrubbing program and deleted the uploads. Then with a final code and click, he deleted the scrubbing program itself.

He walked through the basement hall like an outline of a person. Hollow on the inside. He felt the ceilings and walls closing in on him in a suffocating embrace.

He messaged his great friend and waited in the dim lights of the tunnel, like a ghost king in his collapsing castle. He waited until his legs ached, but he was accustomed to that ache from his long cases.

Like a traveler turning the corner of a long and winding road home, Harry appeared at the end the tunnel. Walking slowly like he didn't have a care in the world. Walking like he was somebody in love.

Harry made his way down the tunnel, "What is it, Shiv?" It's the middle of the afternoon, and I'm busy."

"I think I know what's going on with the prints."

"Really! What's your theory?"

"I'll show you."

Harry followed him into the decontamination suite. Inside, the conveyor belt was moving slowly as Sorter evaluated the prints.

Shiv paused and said more loudly than he'd intended. "Did you really love her."

"Shiv, come on that was so long ago. Let it go."

"Did you?"

Harry stared at him with his watery blue eyes, and he smiled in pure contentment, a smile that Shiv had never known his entire life. "I did, Shiv. She was your wife, always. And you guys were great together. But I did love her, and I think she did love me in her own way."

Shiv nodded and smiled, but his heart cracked like an egg tossed onto the pavement.

Sorter's beak lifted from the conveyor belt as it sensed the intrusion. The avian robot was measuring, surveying its domain. Now it detected the intruder. It swiveled quickly. Its long pincer moving back and forth like the beak of a heron ready to spear a fish. It extended its shining aluminum body towards where Harry stood. It paused and processed. What it had detected was unmistakable. Corruption. A threat to its body prints. A threat to living.

And the beak descended, passing through the open space between Harry's collar and head. And Harry's broad nostalgic smile contorted and his mouth half-opened as his beautiful, perfect child tore through him.

Shiv closed his eyes right as it happened. He couldn't bear to watch. He stumbled backwards and hit the wall headfirst. He crawled out to the hallway in a daze. He didn't have the courage to look back at the crime he'd just orchestrated.

All anger, betrayal, hope, obsession, desperation vanished and what was left was void. He'd spent his life saving lives, healing others, and now in the twilight of age, he'd lost it all. He became numb. He became white and pale like his mimic.

The security arrived quickly. Then the police. In just an hour, detectives, officers, technologists flooded the hospital basement and print lab. After his interviews, Shiv sat, voiceless and alone on a metal bench.

The video feeds were reviewed. The machine malfunction was noted. They kept everyone on the hospital grounds overnight, but nothing could be traced to why Sorter had malfunctioned and who might have been at fault.

After two weeks of investigations, the print lab was back online. Patients needed to be treated and prints produced.

The interim print lab director was a basic science researcher without much by way of organizational skills. After the authorities let up on their investigation, Shiv found a way to procure and use the director's codes to print out Penelope's two remaining prints.

Shiv didn't attend Harry's funeral and his estranged family didn't conduct a proper wake. He'd been the man behind the scenes so there were no flowers and notes from patients and families, but at least the hospital administration gave him a long tribute, a golden brick in the entranceway, and his name engraved on a bench where he'd liked to sit in the healing garden.

Penelope's prints healed, and she remained cancer free. Her body was now entirely intact. She was literally a new woman.

Shiv returned home on a Thursday late afternoon. As he reached the creaky porch he paused in the doorway and heard music. He thought about how lovely it should have felt to hear music from your house after returning from work, but he felt nothing remotely lovely at all.

He stepped into the foyer. There were pairs of loafers, dress shoes, sandals, furry boots, all with the unmistakable smell of old leather. He looked at his own worn gray Crocs and tattered slacks and wondered what it would feel like to bring home the scent of a bakery, cookies, and fresh bread. Or even an office that smelled of ink and paper. Or the funk of an old school and grimy kids. Today he brought home no scent at all. He brought with him the whispers of the dying. He brought home the whisper of Harry's murder. He brought home the whisper of Harry's love for her that wouldn't fade away.

Inside, the recessed lights flooded the living room. The white sheets were off the furniture, and colorful pillows and blankets rested comfortably on chairs and couches. Willow jumped, his little pig legs gyrating his furry body. There was a pot of boiling noodles on the stove along with diced up onions, warm bread, and a rotisserie chicken.

"You went out to get groceries?"

"Delivery, Shiv. I know how to use a computer. I got you dinner. Boiling some spaghetti."

"That's wonderful that you are feeling that well."

"I'm finally *feeling* again. I'm not just your patient anymore."

He stiffened. "You were never *just* my patient."

Her stare was probing. He immediately knew something was troubling her, and it wasn't cancer or missing body parts anymore.

"Now, that you're better, we will need to make plans. We can find a place to start over. You've been trapped in that basement all year. But we need to be careful."

"Very careful indeed."

He cocked his head quizzically.

She fished out the seasoned noodles from a colander and slid over a plate to Shiv. He marveled at how well she was moving. Just a slight limp. Her body seemed to be infused with newfound energy.

He stared at the plate of food. She'd fixed him dinner for the first time in two years, but he still felt nothing. He felt no love, no joy. When he closed his eyes too long all he could see was Sorter's wicked beak.

"I hadn't heard from Harry in a couple weeks. His emails to me just stopped. Then I happened to check the local news, and I read about what happened."

"It was so tragic. I was going to tell you, but I was waiting until you got stronger," Shiv said.

"There's never been a malfunction in the print lab in thirty years. So strange that it would happen now."

"So strange."

"How could you? How could you!"

Shiv recoiled and through the numbness surged regret and shame. He stared down at the plate of food and felt slightly nauseous.

"He was our friend!"

Shiv felt his thoughts jumble and accelerate into explanations and justifications. "I did what I had to do. I did it for you."

"No, Shiv, you did this for *you*."

"Simply, not true. I knew we needed more prints. I knew the ribcage wasn't healthy. The perfusion was not good. It was the final step. I couldn't let Harry stop us again." The words came out without any feeling; the words came out to protect him from feeling.

"Oh, Shiv." Her expression turned sad. "You've done everything to heal me. You succeeded. And I am grateful at another chance to live."

"See. You understand!"

"But not with you, Shiv."

He lifted his head and stared into her soft eyes.

"The man I knew has faded away."

"I'm, I'm- not fine."

"I know. And I can't save you."

His head dropped and he didn't bother trying to hide his dejection.

"The darkness that you created is yours alone."

His entire face felt like it was trembling. In her amber eyes, he saw pity. The friendship and love were gone. His obsession had gone wild, like an underworld demon that had distorted him into its misguided God.

"Harry gave me a lot. He gave me things that I needed to survive as your wife. And you've always known that. I've arranged a proper wake since nobody else did. He should have his legacy honored at the hospital. I'll do that for him."

"You can't be seen there."

"Oh, I won't, but you can go and honor him."

He nodded.

"You've lost something that you can't ever get back. You can't *ever* work at ReStart again. Those hands can no longer be responsible for life and death. You've gone too far."

Shiv raised his hands, arthritic and knobby that all at once looked aged beyond repair.

"I am grateful for how much you sacrificed for me, for how much we sacrificed for each other, but I can't save you anymore. I don't know if you can be saved. I'm going to go for a walk just to the end of the block and back. I got some new running shoes. This body is young and fresh now."

"Will you come back?"

"I will today. But one day, very soon, I won't. I'll run out that door and start my life over, somewhere I won't be discovered, and you won't ever see me again."

She left him with his untouched plate of food and laced up her sparkly white running shoes. She threw open the front doors and the red light of dusk blasted her body, and she made her way back out into the world, while Shiv sat with his mutated dog and saw only the darkness lurking behind the sunset.

ABOUT THE AUTHOR

Rajeev Prasad is a physician who lives with his wife, three kids, and a very cute dog in Northern California. His stories have appeared in *The Magazine of Fantasy and Science Fiction, Clarkesworld,* and several other markets. He thanks you for reading this story.

The Weight of Your Own Ashes
CARLIE ST. GEORGE

Alice wants to hold a funeral for me, which is disconcerting because I'm not dead. But humans, like all aliens—and certainly all single-forms—have their own idiosyncrasies.

I'm used to the idiosyncrasies, of course: I've lived on Earth—in my tertiary body, at least—since my hatching in San Francisco, grew up in a cramped apartment in North Beach and am very much a Californian, an American, and an Earthling, if not a human. (I refuse the terms Earther and Terran, which may be in fashion but have no charm.) I can't pretend it was always easy growing up here, and humans do have specific biological quirks that will forever baffle me: sweat, for one, and also the garbled hallucinations more commonly referred to as dreams. But despite its many abhorrent flaws, Earth—like any other world—also has its small joys, its thousand little wonders that you simply can't find anywhere else. Garlic bread, for instance, and dim sum. Butterflies. Magnolia trees. Trick-or-treating. Kandinsky paintings. It's my culture, just not my only culture. My home, my life—but only one of four.

Well. One of three, now.

Three weeks ago, I died in a catastrophic bus accident on my way to UC Berkeley; simultaneously, I was hibernating on Myr in my primary body, hibernating on Banquo in my quinary body, and meal prepping on the *Valorous Raccoon* in my secondary body. (The literal name of *Valorous Raccoon* is closer to *Scavenger Animal That is Righteously Courageous*, but more often than not, I prefer my own translations.) Dying has a way of grabbing your full attention; for several minutes, I lost all awareness of my secondary body before forcefully slamming back into it. Fortunately, shock allowed me the emotional distance needed to compose two Earthbound messages: one to my doctoral advisor, apologizing for not making our meeting, and one to Alice, reminding her not to worry—yes, my tertiary body had died, but I was fine and already working on travel arrangements back to Earth, and if she could just make sure my remains—whatever was left of them—were delivered to a reputable alien-friendly mortuary, I would handle everything else. Then, instead of making those arrangements, I had a small breakdown on the galley floor when my captain walked in and, concerned, asked if I was okay.

But that was weeks ago. I'm feeling much better now. It's Alice who's struggling, really.

I knew there would be *some* awkwardness, of course, especially as my bodies vary in form. I'd wanted to leave Banquo behind, considering the only thing I'd miss about that icy hell-rock was Jwa—but my quinary body is a fraternal body, for lack of a better English term: male, with a brightly feathered crown, and noticeably shorter than my female forms—which *are* identical, save the odd injury, cosmetic choice, and level of sun exposure. It'd be . . . easier for everyone, I told myself, if I left the *Valorous Raccoon* instead. Alice, especially, might have trouble recognizing me as *me* if I suddenly showed up as a man—and I would be a man because I use male pronouns in that body. (Some well-meaning human friends have described me as trans, but I'm not entirely convinced the label fits and often find difficulty translating my gender in English, despite having spoken the language all my life. Simultaneously living in several different bodies and cultures means simultaneously experiencing several different gender norms and expressions, and it can be difficult to translate those multi-bodied experiences to fit a single-form's conceptions and expectations of gender.)

The primary differences between my secondary and tertiary bodies are these: tattoos (my secondary body has none), skin color (milk white rather than a near-human alabaster), crown and cape colors (red and white feathers rather than black and white), and a significant limp (my left hip is slightly fucked from a fall that my tertiary body never experienced). Otherwise, my features are identical, my weight very similar, my eyes still round and dark. I stopped wearing my dark eye makeup in favor of neutrals, my tank tops and coveralls in favor of vests and plaids. I don't look like some long-lost sister. I look like *Yonder.* I look like *me.*

But Alice doesn't see me anymore.

We met years ago in grad school. Same field of study, cultural xenology, but with different focuses: Alice's primary interest is culinary traditions, whereas my dissertation—if I ever finish it—is on comparative ghost stories. There are a surprising number of non-humans in the program, given Earth's rather dismal non-human population, but I'm the only Myriad student at UC Berkeley, and it can be . . . disheartening to see how even other species react when they realize I'm not single-bodied like them. It's not like junior high, at least—we're all too horrifically busy for that sort of active bullying; instead, it's the casual slur, the occasional shudder, the inappropriate question, or wildly incorrect assumption that would be insulting from anybody, but is *especially* egregious from other xenology students—and often faculty, too.

Alice, though, has always been different. Her immediate questions were not about masturbation, nor did she play devil's advocate to "prove" that I was a liar, deluded, or inorganic; mostly, her questions were about food. Alice made me comfortable. Alice made me laugh, and when I eventually did share pictures of my other bodies, Alice looked at them with wonder, rather than horror, and I thought—I really thought—

Dying is no small thing. I never expected it to be easy. But when I stepped off the shuttle, when I finally got through customs and saw her again with my own two eyes . . . I thought Alice would hold me. I thought she would say my name and cling.

Instead, Alice flinched and looked away.

Now I'm here, standing in my living room, holding my own urn.

"It's not right," Alice says from behind me. "She—I mean, *you*—you *died*. It's not fair that you won't let me mourn."

Is that what I'm doing? It doesn't feel like it. I've never thought of myself as controlling before. It's not the kind of person I want to be—who am I, to dictate someone else's heart?

Still, what is there to mourn? I'm *here*.

This isn't the first time I've died. It's the second—or fourth, depending how you count. My biological mother laid seven eggs, but one never hatched, and another was obliterated when a fire destroyed an entire incubation center. Thankfully, the other eggs were scattered throughout the stars: there's a reason Myriads say *scatter the nests or shatter the shells*—a proverb usually translated as *don't put all your eggs in one basket*, but again, this lacks poetry.

I can't remember my egg deaths, but I *do* remember dying as a child: a devastating illness swept through my lunar colony, causing terrible skin sores and mouth lesions. All my feathers fell out, and I remember hibernating as much as possible: the doctors had hoped it would heal my quaternary body, though at the time, I was mostly concerned with avoiding the pain. Unfortunately, dying often triggers a kind of hypnagogic jerk, a last-ditch survival reflex, so rather than sleeping through my death, well. One moment I was awake in my tertiary body, playing tag with my siblings in Washington Square—and in the next, I was *also* awake on that far-off moon, bleeding from my gums and writhing from a terrible, crushing agony as my two tiny hearts gave out. *I'm scared*, I remember thinking, as blurry hands and faces frantically rushed around me. *It hurts; I'm SCARED*—

And then my quaternary body died, and I was back in San Francisco again, on hands and knees in the dirt, gasping, with my littlest sibling, Gray, screaming their head off for our parents.

Was I cremated back then? I don't know. It doesn't matter so much, only—it's a strange thing, to see your own remains, to know the weight of your own ashes.

"It doesn't have to be a human funeral," Alice says, more gently. "You know that, right?"

I do. Alice has proved more than willing to participate in customs both outside her own specific upbringing (white, Protestant, Upper West Side) and outside the greater human culture in general (largely isolationist, and . . . rural, for lack of a better word). We've tried so many new things together: Martian séance festivals, galactic liquor tastings, the perplexingly named orbital bungee jump (*never* do this). Alice has always been curious, respectful, game for anything. If I wanted to hold a specifically Myriad funeral, I'm sure she would willingly participate.

But that's not the problem. The problem is—outside of a few frankly strange religious denominations—Myriads don't *have* funerals for their tertiary bodies, or *any* body save the final one. The whole idea of it is . . . odd. Unsettling. Like having a funeral for an amputated limb.

"Actually," Alice says, when I tell her this. "There *are* humans who bury lost limbs."

Disconcerting. Not the practice, itself, but the fact that I've lived here my whole life and never knew that: never been to a leg funeral, never read a single story where a character's limb was laid to rest—or, better yet, became a haunted limb because it *wasn't* laid to rest. I could live until I'm a hundred and sixty and still miss so much of the world. It fills me with dread, somedays; I don't know how single-bodied species handle it. At least, I have four bodies to walk with, see with, taste with.

Had. I had four bodies.

Yes, there's something to mourn. There's something for *me* to mourn, but Alice—

"Anyway," Alice says, "this isn't just an arm, Y—you know. It's your *body*. It *died*."

I remember, I almost snap, because I *do* remember—pinned, bleeding, and extremely conscious when the bus went up in flames. *I'm scared, it hurts, I'm SCARED*, and then—

Boom.

But that's not the problem, either. It's not that I died, because I'm still alive. It's not the annoying dash of existentialism, the useless smidgeon of trauma. Those things, I can manage. Badly, perhaps, but I can handle them.

But Alice won't say my name anymore, and I don't know how to handle that at all.

I start to argue, but Alice begins crying again, and it's just . . . easier, ultimately, to compromise. That's what relationships are, right? I need to be reasonable about this. No, I won't do a large ceremony. Yes, we can do a sea service. Yes, Alice can say a few words while I scatter the gray clumps of my tertiary body to the water below.

What Alice says, weeping:

"Yonder, I love you. I miss you."

Like she's alone by the water. Like I'm a ghost, after all.

The next few weeks are . . . difficult.

Alice is avoiding me, which is challenging, considering that we live together. She stares at me, but won't *look* at me. She'll speak to me, but never touch me. Sex isn't an issue, fortunately, as we rarely bother fucking anyway: Alice is a "sex is fine, but what about tiramisu" ace, and my sex drive only kicks in twice a year. But I already miss holding her. I miss how softly she pets my feathers. I miss snuggling close while watching some whodunnit, exchanging increasingly outlandish theories and laughing into her shoulder whenever we're both wrong.

Everyone reacts differently to traumatic events. I'm trying to imagine this from Alice's point of view, which is difficult because Alice will only ever die once. That scares me, if I think about it too much. It's not just her, either: Gray, my *VR* crew. My human parents, who I already lost. Our relationship was . . . complicated . . . but when they died, that was it: no second chances.

When I think about losing Alice like that, I ache to grasp her tightly with both hands and feet. But Alice doesn't need that. She needs time, space. I can give her that. I can stop being selfish and give her that.

"I swear to Christ, if you call yourself selfish one more time," Gray says.

Gray is my only sibling who still lives in the Bay Area. There are five of us, all adopted: Gray is the youngest, human and Chinese American, and dresses in whatever historical fashion they're interested in at the time: lately, it's all dyed mullets and bright colors, very queer glam rock. We had little in common as children, but as adults, we've bonded over a bitter and grief-struck love for parents who raised us, loved us, but wouldn't accept our names. (It's not quite the same, of course: I don't consider Felicity a deadname. I did once have five given names, after all, and unlike Gray, it doesn't hurt me to hear them—but choosing one or more for yourself *is* an important Myriad rite of passage, and the fact that my human parents found that disrespectful, inconsequential—that *did* hurt.)

Gray is here providing moral support via empanadas while I focus on my other post-death problems: paperwork. There is an unholy amount of it. This would be true even if I was simply and irrevocably dead, America being a melting pot of bureaucratic nightmares, but is wildly complicated by my status as both living and non-living. Three bodies, one consciousness! How is that so difficult? It's not like state, federal, and planetary governments haven't had time to prepare! First Contact (between our species, at least) was over ninety years ago, and yet here we are—with forms for new ID cards and new health insurance and even national *and* global visa applications because, suddenly, it's become unclear if I count as either a US or Earth citizen, as my secondary body—this body—was born on a planet in the distant Red Fox galaxy.

"So, you're trying to keep from getting deported *off-planet*," Gray says, "and your girlfriend can't even bother hugging you cause you've got red feathers and a limp now?"

"No ink, either," I say, too bitterly. All week, Alice had kept fetching me cardigans, even though Earth still feels very warm in this body. I'd assumed it was residual anxiety, overprotectiveness—Alice has always had something of a sweetly chivalrous streak. Turns out, she's simply discomfited by the sight of my bare arms.

Be fair, I remind myself. "It's complicated."

"It's weak," Gray says. "*She's* weak."

I smile. Gray has always been stubborn, bull-hearted, righteously indignant. As a child, I'd found those qualities very tedious; now, I love them for it. "It must be strange," I force myself to say, reluctantly. "Seeing me this way, for her *and* for you—"

Gray leans back. The flat line of their red mouth speaks annoyance. The high lift of their red eyebrow says *bitch, remember to whom you speak.*

I laugh. Still. "It's not the same, and you know it. When you used to have nightmares—"

"Ugh, you *promised* to stop bringing that up—"

"I didn't hold you with these arms," I remind them. "When we played tag, I wasn't in this body. You've never held these hands before. Can you honestly say—"

"Yes," Gray says, and immediately takes my hand.

I stop.

"Sure," Gray says. "It's strange. So? Who gives a shit? Lots of things are strange for a while, and then we get used to them—or else we stay limited and narrow and fucking sad."

Gray's grip is firm and reassuring, and I swallow, unexpectedly emotional. I've missed this; I've really missed someone else touching this skin. Desperately, I will my body not to do anything weird, like grip Gray's hand even tighter, or—God help me—cry. "I'm trying. I'm really trying to give Alice time to—"

"No," Gray says. "This isn't new behavior. Alice has always been limited."

I frown. That's not true. Alice is open, adventurous. Alice and I are partners; we *grow* together—I thought we did, at least. "That's not what you said when she moved in with me. *And then they were roommates,* you said."

"Yeah, cause you're my sister, and I'll support you even when you make lousy decisions with your heart—but I haven't *liked* Alice since she refused to go meet your *Raccoon* fam."

I wince. "It's complicated," I say, which is annoying because I'm repeating excuses. "She *did* want to meet them," I say, which has the benefit of being true. "I don't know how you got the idea that Alice is some sort of bigot, but—"

Gray waves their free hand. "Yeah, whatever, she's probably not a *horrible* person. But come on. You always worry about her feelings. When does she worry about yours?"

That's not true, either. Is it? Doesn't Alice worry about me?

Gray lets go of my hand, and—entirely without meaning to—I grab them again, clinging. Then *I* try to pull back, embarrassed—but Gray refuses to let go.

"She loves me," I say, and hate how uncertain my voice sounds. She *does* love me, a version of me, but maybe—

"Okay," Gray says, the unspoken words clear: *if you say so.* "But Yonder . . . does she *know* you?"

And I can't answer the question.

• • •

I do eventually make a solid dent in the paperwork and set up an appointment with an immigration lawyer. Gray helps (the empanadas do, too), but by the time they leave, my hip has gone stiff, and the stress and frustration has built into a deep ache between my shoulder blades. I take a mild painkiller, turn on some Vivaldi (Nisi Dominus, to be specific), and collapse onto my bed, whilst simultaneously waking up my primary and quinary bodies. I stare up at three different ceilings: taupe (here), brick red (Banquo), and something close to fuchsia (Myr). A few weeks ago, I would have seen gunmetal gray, too, and I miss it, the *Valorous Raccoon*. I even miss things I used to hate, like the gravity going haywire and rebooting in the middle of meal prep, all my diced vegetables floating—and then all my diced vegetables fucked.

I might never see my canteen again if I stay in this body in this life.

But I made my choice, didn't I? Music keeps me from wallowing: I turn on some chime-pop on Banquo and grunge-hymns on Myr and listen to the wondrous mesh of discordant melodies, a habit that Alice has always found strange. *Isn't it jarring*, she asks, and it can be—loud, unpleasant, overwhelming. But you can also create such *symphonies*, and there can be such lovely surprises, too, when a chant, a clacking, and a lullaby synchronize into something unlikely and transcendent. I love art that is created this way, collages and remixes of . . . anything, really: music, monologues, poetry, prayer, color. There's a beauty in capturing multiple sensations over space and time—and, it should go without saying, drugs are best experienced like this, too.

I hate listening to multiple conversations, Alice says, and it's true: Myriads are more biologically suited to that sort of thing: I can hold multiple conversations at once, provided they're simple enough, and complete multiple small tasks, so long as they don't require any serious focus. Most things do require focus, of course, and so mostly I alternate bodies—but there is a *glory* in these small moments of being fully awake as no single-bodied can be.

Hey, Alice sometimes says—no, she's saying it right now. "Hey."

I sit up. Alice is leaning in the bedroom doorway, watching me fondly. No, wistfully—with love, yes, but also with loss.

Alice sits beside me. On Banquo and Myr, I turn down the music. I could go back into hibernation, but I don't want to; I don't *feel* like it. I feel—

Hip-sore (here). Hungry (Myr). Thirsty (Banquo). Cold (Banquo). Frustrated (everywhere). Anxious (everywhere). Tired (everywhere).

Alice, very tentatively, takes my hand. My breath catches.

"I know it's been . . . difficult lately," she says. "That I've been distant. I'm sorry."

I exhale, squeezing her hand gently. She smiles a little, squeezing back.

"It's just—"

No. No, don't ruin it—

"I feel like I'm cheating on her," Alice says. "On you."

Immediately, I want to pull my hand back. I don't, but on Banquo, I get up and stare out the window. Another snowstorm, white and wild. I resist the melodramatic urge to walk into it.

"You aren't," I tell Alice. "I'm not a different person. I'm just—"

"I *know*," Alice says, sharp. "I'm just telling you how I *feel*."

I know how you *feel*, I think, unfair and bitter—but then, maybe it isn't so unfair. Maybe Gray was right, at least a little; why *are* Alice's feelings always prioritized over mine?

On Myr, I walk to the window, too. Clear, pink skies, and three visible moons.

"*I* feel like you're leaving me," I tell Alice.

"I'm not—"

"You're never around," I say, and inside, some resentful dam bursts. "Even when you're here, you're not. You keep treating me like I'm fucking *gone*—"

"I don't—"

"They could deport me, Alice! Do you understand that? Do you care how *I* feel because *I'm* terrified all the time, of losing my home, losing you, even taking the goddamn bus now—"

Abruptly, Alice turns away. "I don't want to talk about that."

"Well, what if *I* need to?" I yell, forcing her to face me. "Do I have to handle everything on my own? The paperwork, the loneliness, the memories. You know I remember it, right? This body didn't bleed, but *I* bled; *I* saw the flames; I *felt* it when—"

But Alice only says, "I *can't*," and leaves, slamming the front door behind her.

I collapse back on the mattress, closing my eyes. There's a window here, too, but I don't bother looking out. I'm too exhausted to get up, and anyway, it's not the window or view I want it to be. Too many city lights, and I ache to see stars.

So, I go see the stars.

I wait until the blizzard on Banquo passes; then I leave my secondary body behind and gear up, venturing out to find a nice, isolated snow hill—

excellent for stargazing, quiet conversations, and very cold picnicking, assuming you don't need oxygen to breathe, which, of course, I do. Jwa, however, does not.

Jwa is less a friend than a fate-bound, a term he finds superstitious and sentimental because he is, and always has been, a cantankerous little shit. We first met as children on that lunar colony; we both died on that lunar colony, too. I lost contact with him and everyone else I'd loved there—my parents, my teachers, my friends—because children rarely get to make their own choices, and all my *other* parents decided I needed a clean break to move on. But that break had been devastating; it had been anything but clean, and I remember longing for adulthood because it meant that nobody could ever make those choices for me again.

(I wouldn't go back to being a child, not for anything, but lately I wonder if maybe I'm just shit at making the right choices for myself.)

Running into Jwa last year—in this frozen truck stop of a planet, no less—well, those were astronomical odds, miracle odds, and to hell with what he says about it. We've never had very much in common, anyway, save our shared bleak history, and also this: Jwa is Untold, the only other multiple-body species that I know of. (The actual English exonym is Untoldan, but that's so ungainly; I prefer the root word.) Unlike me, Jwa has ninety-seven identical bodies, all of which look rather like a hickory horned devil caterpillar, if those caterpillars were faceless, translucent, the size of a human arm, and beaded with one hundred and twenty dark eyes. Ninety-seven bodies *is* rather high for his species, but extremely typical of Jwa, who's always had to win absolutely everything.

Case in point: "You wouldn't see *me* wasting around on a planet where I can't even breathe the air."

And: "I've only lost *one* body, unlike *some* people I could mention."

And: "I *told* you to stop fucking that puffed up amputation."

Amputation is likely the handheld's best approximation at some derogatory word for *single-bodied*. We often rely on translator apps; I prefer not to, but the Untold communicate entirely by colored flushes and secretions, which I'm as biologically incapable of producing as Jwa is unable to process vocal speech. We make it work for us: Jwa can usually decipher the rough meaning of my hand gestures, and I can work out his general mood by whatever color he's oozing. Currently, his bodies—there are four of them—are coated in dots of rose-pink goo, which means he's a little sad/sorry/pitying, but mostly smug as hell.

With effort, I bite back on a lecture about allonormative assumptions. "No," I tell him. "You said not to date *any* single-bodied person because you're conventional and boring."

"Because I'm not a reckless idiot," Jwa insists, flushing an indignant buttercup.

This is an old argument: Jwa thinks most Myriads are reckless idiots for spreading themselves out across the universe; in turn, I think *he's* an idiot for wasting so much precious life in a solitary collective. If he'd lived this way as a child, he wouldn't be around now to brag about having only died once. *Scatter the nests*, I told him, to which he'd asked, *is it still a nest with only one twig*, and I'd said something very cutting and mature like *fuck off* because, really, we just bring out the worst in each other.

Today I'm prepared with several choice insults—but then Jwa flushes a bitter forest green and says, "They see us as bugs."

Well. Yes. Despite his obvious sentience, some humans probably *would* see Jwa as a bug, just like some caw and jeer at me, asking if my father fucked a Northern cardinal. "Humans—"

"Not just humans," Jwa interrupts. "*All* amputations. And not just me. Not just bugs."

"I don't—"

"Bots," Jwa says. "Clones. Monsters. Parasites. Non-people. Non-sentients. *Less* than."

Demons, I think, despite myself, not because I often actually get called a demon, but because the true English exonym for my species is Legion, not Myriad—and that absolutely was *not* chosen as an allusion to the ancient Romans. It infuriates me when I think about it, so I try not to think about it. I try to enjoy my silent rebellions, my superior translations; I try not to be consumed by my anger, but—

"We frighten them," Jwa continues, greener than I've ever seen him. "We're *more* than them, so they make us less. They can feel justified that way: we're less, so we don't matter."

I think of middle school, then, and the casual slurs I still hear, and all the single-bodied people who've shuddered when they realized just how different I am. Every species in every world across the whole universe is the same: fearful and hateful and *small*.

But I don't let it consume me; I won't, because—

Individual *people*—not bodies, but *people*—aren't all so limited or sad. Individual people—like Gray, like Jwa—are small, sentient wonders of their own. You can meet them and learn them and hate them and touch them and watch the bright, beautiful stars on a tiny, white world with them. You can change them and be changed by them, too. Sometimes for the better, sometimes for the worse.

Alice is her own sentient wonder. But are we really changing each other for the better? How can we be, if she doesn't see me? *Did* she ever really see me?

I still don't know. I want to think so. But I look at Jwa and his four green-glowing bodies; I look at the stars and think of my *VR* crew—

And I think, yes, I already made my choice. But it's never too late to make a better one.

When Alice gets home, I tell her, "I think you should meet my other bodies."

Alice actually stops mid-step. "I'm sure I will," she says, with an unconvincing smile.

"No, I mean soon. After everything . . . I think it's important."

Because I'd told myself it was complicated, that I shouldn't read too much into it—Alice had already seen the pictures, and she hadn't been upset then—but the truth is Alice *had* been excited about meeting my Raccoon fam. She didn't back out because she was uncomfortable with *them*. It was only when she remembered the crew also included *me*, that—for the very first time—she'd be in the same space with *two* of me: cooking, talking, holding her hands . . .

That's when Alice backed out of the trip.

"Okay," Alice says now. "But let me hit this deadline first."

"Sure," I tell her—but once that deadline passes and Alice comes up with another excuse, I secretly begin the dual journeys back to Earth. Banquo is a quick portal hop, but Myr takes six, and two of those portals are notorious for traffic backups and passport fuckups. I hibernate through much of the journey, and in the meantime, catch up on my dissertation reading; in the meantime, update my immigration lawyer; in the meantime, live in the stilted quiet with Alice.

And then finally, it's time.

"Alice," I say, stepping into the kitchen. "My other bodies are here now. They're coming up the elevator."

The coffee mug slips out of Alice's hand, rattling against the countertop. "What? But we said—and I'm not dressed—"

"I can already see you," I remind her.

"Well . . . I *know* that, but look, we said we'd wait."

"Yes. And then you kept postponing."

Alice crosses her arms. "You *know* how hard it's been lately. If you just—"

"Alice," I interrupt, as patiently as I can. "I don't actually need your permission to come into my own home in my own bodies."

Alice visibly wrestles with that.

"I just don't think it's a good idea," she says after a moment, not looking at me.

"Okay. Why not?"

"Well, I just . . . I don't know if I'm *comfortable* with that. I mean . . . " She flounders. "I know they're all you, but it's just . . . "

Weird, she wants to say. Or *creepy*. Or *fucked up*. Or *you seem so neat in theory, but only if I don't think about it too much.*

"I don't care," I tell her. I punch in the door code with my primary body and follow my primary body inside with my quinary body.

Alice freezes.

I walk over, stand beside myselves: three Yonders, all in a row. Maybe I could be mistaken for identical twin sisters and their brightly feathered kid brother, but that's not who I am. That'll never be who I am.

"I know you didn't want this," I tell her. "But I need you to see me, Alice."

"I do!" Alice says, eyes watery. "But this is just so—"

"Do you?" I interrupt, this time with my primary body, "or have you—"

"Been pretending that I'm some human with feathers." I run my hand through my secondary crown. "Because—"

"I'm not human," I say with my quinary body. "I was never human. I was never single-bodied. This is me. This is all me. The scattered ash—"

"And this—"

"And this. Each is *me*, Alice. I'm Yonder, your Yonder, and I'll—"

"Never be human," I say, simultaneously with all of my bodies—

And Alice shudders.

And I know.

At first, Alice waits for me to pack my bags.

And then she keeps waiting.

And then she waits some more until finally, she realizes I have no intention of packing anything. This is *my* apartment. She moved in with *me*.

"But . . . you aren't *staying*," Alice says, and it takes me a moment to understand what she means. She isn't just talking about this building; she means UC Berkeley, the doctorate program, Earth. With three bodies and four lives, surely this is the one I'm leaving behind. She's waiting for me, I realize, to take my bodies and go home.

But I *am* home. I was born here, and even if I hadn't been—this is where I chose to build my future, and no one, certainly not my new ex-girlfriend, will take that choice from me. I long to tell Alice that; I want to be cold, confident, devastating. But I'm still too heartsick, and eventually, I just point at the front door, watching Alice close it behind her with a quiet click.

And that's it. It's over.

I do cry, then, in all my bodies, even, because it's always difficult saying goodbye, even if the person you're saying goodbye to isn't the person you thought—and especially when you've had to say goodbye a lot, recently. (I'd told Jwa my decision before I left Banquo. He'd gone silent, glowing mournful blue approval. Then, quickly turning pastel pink and condescending: *Finally. I thought you'd NEVER figure your shit out.*)

(I'd dumped snow on him and promised we'd meet again. We will. I'm sure of it.)

Eventually, though, I get tired of crying, and annoyed at myself, and pretty hungry, too, so I start chopping vegetables with my secondary body, while I clap my quinary hands to gospel-EDM, and lean out the open window in my primary form, listening to breaking glass and laughing people and a neighbor singing a Spanish love song. Tomorrow, I'll have appointments to keep (my immigration lawyer is *not* thrilled with how I keep causing her more paperwork), and also messages to send, travel arrangements to make, dissertations to work on, siblings to hold hands with—

But tonight, I just want to sit back and unwind, comfortable in all my skins. Tonight, I'll listen to the joyous small symphonies of my apartment, my neighborhood, my world.

ABOUT THE AUTHOR

Carlie St. George is a speculative writer and Shirley Jackson Award finalist from Northern California. Her debut short story collection *You Fed Us to the Roses* is available from Robot Dinosaur Press. Her short fiction has been published in magazines such as *Nightmare, Lightspeed,* and *PseudoPod,* as well as in multiple Best of Year anthologies. When not writing, she's usually obsessing over television, obsessing over fanfic, or negotiating with her monster cats. (She's losing.)

Our Father

K. J. KHAN

I think of you most when the sun sets on Atlas.

The skies are so bright there you can feel the colors on your skin.

I find myself repeating this to my granddaughter, Lila. The night she was born, I took her onto the terrace to watch the daylight roll back in waves. We stood together in the rosy light and she waved her chubby hands, transfixed. I've heard infants can't see color, but I think she did.

Watch, Quin. I remember you pulling me onto your lap so I could be nearer the screen as it changed, my fingers raised overhead to catch color. *See? And every night, the colors will be different.* I could smell the stale sweat on your shirt—you were self-conscious, I now know, about how little we bathed on the ship. But I loved to curl up on your chest; your scent, like your breath, comforted me. We coveted that spot, my seven siblings and I, and we argued so endlessly you were forced to schedule out snuggles.

Then again, we argued over everything, didn't we?

Ai, you would sigh, when we came tumbling in over whose turn it was to choose our meals or sleep in the topmost bunk. *Niños, what have I told you? Ask Archie.* And that would settle it. There was no point trying to argue with him. Trey would try—of course he would—asking question after question, about why we should listen to an android, or to anyone, or who made rules in the first place. Archie would answer, wandering further and further into abstraction, but in the end he always came back to his programming.

Because Javi said so, Trey. And because nine humans cannot share such close quarters without some rules.

Lila drew a picture of the *Horizon* yesterday. You would like it—each room in the ship a different color, the proportions made thick and unruly by crayon. I've told her about the track you made for us, and she's sketched the route in red dashes. Up and down the corridors, looping around the concourse (under some dining tables and over others), even squeezing into the ductwork, in the places where it was safe to do so. I can picture you now, timing us as we ran in little heats of two, and then writing our fastest runs on our handmade scoreboard.

Lila asks questions about the *Horizon* every time she visits. She plays games about being aboard it, where the food comes in tiny, dehydrated cubes, and the beds are lofted on top each other, so that every night is "like camping." She doesn't believe we could ever be bored, in such a paradise.

We had a VR room, but there were only two headsets that had to be shared between us. I remember playing on the concourse with Prim, waiting our turn, the day the man appeared.

He walked past the dining area and we froze, mid-game, mid-word. Prim started to whimper until I took her hand.

The man turned to where we crouched beneath a table. Surprise registered on his puffy, sallow face (*like a mushroom,* Prim said). He smiled.

Hello. He must have thought his tone sounded friendlier than it did. *I'm looking for Javier.*

You were angry when we arrived with him. You tried to hide it, but we knew by your eyes, by the stiff way you pulled him into your quarters. We could hear the conversation from outside the closed door.

What are you doing here, Gordon? I'm supposed to come check in with you, not the other way around.

You weren't there.

What, you can't wait two minutes? You've startled them.

They don't know I'm on the ship?

They know you're onboard. Not that you wake up and walk around. Shouldn't be hard to explain.

What?

Suspended animation.

Your voice took on a tone we'd never heard before. *You think that's the hard part to explain?*

The schools still played transmissions from Earth when my daughter was little. Not the worst videos, of course. The age-appropriate ones. But even those upset her.

Why don't they come here? I remember her asking. *They can breathe the air here.*

But it's expensive to immigrate, isn't it? I've seen the ticket prices for the passenger ships, those great cosmic ocean liners where the passengers sleep for all but the final few months. Cheaper by far to fly as the crew, either of a passenger ship or a transport vessel. That is, if you can land such a coveted job.

We still live in a crew neighborhood. We could afford, now, to move to a passenger one, but I doubt we ever will. Crewmembers, to a person, appreciate even the mundane parts of planetary existence. I think it's because they know what it's like, standing inside a sleeping ship. Even if they were only waking once every few months, a day at a time. The voyage wasn't dead space for them. Wasn't wasted time.

Three other men—besides "the man"—slept on the *Horizon*. Three others and the rows and rows of glimmering cases, each one holding its own collection of little cylinders, each cylinder holding what looked like a tiny pink tadpole. It took us a long time to realize what they were, or to notice that each case held a group of eight.

Ship 449, Population Transport, (Year 24 of 50)
Transcript
Property of New Horizons Inc.
Classified

Q. Gordon: Look, we've tried, okay? The pod's broken. They're maturing.
R. Lewis: How far along?
Q. Gordon: Twelve weeks.
R. Lewis: [expletive]
L. Grayson: So what do we do?
Q. Gordon: Flush them.
R. Lewis: We can't do that.
Q. Gordon: Can't we? We've got seven hundred others. Who's going to miss eight? Besides, what are we supposed to feed them?
R. Lewis: The emergency food stores should be enough. It's designed for infants too, in case the colony needed it.
Q. Gordon: That food is supposed to be for US. What if our pods break and WE need it?
L. Grayson: Can't we leave them with Archie? Check in monthly or something?
R. Lewis: You want to leave them with a [expletive] android?
L. Grayson: I don't hear you offering any suggestions.
Q. Gordon: Hernandez? Are you even paying attention?

• • •

I'd known it was work but I had no idea how much, not until my daughter's birth. Four months of broken sleep with her and I started sending in requests to view the *Horizon's* video log. I had to know how you did it, raising eight infants with only an android to help you. The sight of young Javier—the Javier who could have made it to Atlas, if not for us—shocked me. I'd spent years thinking about my own deprivations. But I'd taken your decision for granted; I had somehow forgotten what it cost you.

Do you remember what I asked you? About hating the other crew-members? After all, they could've divided the time. It was already year twenty-four when the pod failed; if each had taken a little over five years, like you suggested, you all would have arrived on Atlas still young.

You smiled that slight, secretive, shy grin. *Is fifty-six so old?*

It is when you've lost twenty-six of those years.

Lost? You stopped walking to look me in the eyes. You had to look up a little to do that now.

Javier Hernandez is paying attention. He is thinking about the notices that used to appear in his hometown, listing the latest hazardous items and contaminated areas to avoid (which no one in the town could afford to do). He is thinking of the day in his late teens when the results of his physical came back marked in red, and how his mother cried when she found out because he was the last, last of six other children who had also received the red mark that meant the end of your bloodline. He sees her throwing out heirlooms that no longer have a purpose, because it is too painful to hold onto clothes that won't ever be filled, toys that won't ever be held. (He has had to lose the past as well as the future to take this post. He didn't want to but his uncle worked so hard to secure the spot, and Javi is the youngest and single and will have the most time to establish himself upon arrival. Too late, of course, to bring along anyone else.) And he is thinking that someone—many someones—signed waivers to send their little zygotes across the universe, creating children they'd never meet so that a wealthy colony could gain some genetic diversity. He looks at the video feed of the incubator pod, watching as the embryos sleep.

J. Hernandez: I have a suggestion.

Atlas was supposed to be your new start. I said. *And you spent it aboard a tiny ship instead. It's not fair. None of it.*

Maybe not. You put your hand on my head, drawing my forehead down to touch yours. *But it wasn't lost, Quin. Never call it lost.*

111

I returned to the video log in the weeks after the memorial service. I noticed something new this time. Though you had programmed Archie to give us our bottles—you would never have slept, otherwise—you still woke at regular intervals. To hold each of us. As often as you could.

Everyone has a color, Lila tells me, holding up her now-finished drawing. *To match the rooms.* There we were: eight little doodle babies, laid out in a circle. And behind us, undrawn, our children, and children's children, and Lila herself and the children she will tell the story to, on and on and on, filling the page, the table, the walls. Pinwheeled around our Papa Javi.

Center of our tiny solar system.

ABOUT THE AUTHOR

K. J. Khan is a writer, artist, and mom from Indiana. (She currently lives in Rhode Island, but has to give her home state its due). Her short fiction has appeared in *Short Edition* and *Mysterion,* and two of her short stories have been featured in the Tangent Online Recommended Reading List for 2021 and 2022. When she's not writing or painting, she enjoys going on adventures with her husband and son.

Hive Minds and Drones: Bees in Space in Real Life and in Science Fictional Cosmos

D.A. XIAOLIN SPIRES

Hive Minds. Colony Queens. Cells. Drones. Flight. Dances. Stings. Buzzing. Quivering. Pheromones. It's no wonder that bees take flight in the human imagination.

Their appeal in science fiction is grounded in their real-life accomplishments and peculiarities: their social organization, anatomy, hive construction and hovering, buzzing flight. And to add to that, *both* honeybees and bumblebees make honey!

Are bees the most charming, cutest, and most charismatic—and possibly dangerous—thanks to their stingers—biological entity, rife with metaphors for a xenobiological lifeform? Possibly, and some authors would say yes, as they've taken inspiration from these fuzzy communal-oriented sweetness-producing flying insects to create sci-fi futures that involve some version of them.

Non-fictional Space Bees

Wait, wait, you say. Non-fiction? And *space bees*? Step on the brakes for a second! Did we discover a colony on the moon or in Alpha Centauri? Are there rivers of honey crisscrossing Mars? Are they out there pollinating wildflowers on an exoplanet?

No, or well, not yet, as far as we're aware. But, space bees have existed and the answer is closer to home because humans have sent bees into space. If you'd like to learn more about that, I'd recommend "Bees in

Space" by Ross Conrad in *Bee Culture: The Magazine of Beekeeping*. It's an informative article about experiments through National Aeronautics and Space Administration (NASA) in conjunction with other institutions, such as the National Science Teaching Association (NSTA), on taking bees into the cosmos. These institutions have a vested interest to see how bees work (or don't . . . work) in space. Different bee-related space missions tackle various aspects worthy of study and these areas include insect flight motion in microgravity, bee nutrition, construction of honeycomb structures while in space, perception of directionality in zero-G and adaptation.

The honeybee was the first bee sent to outer space, though the result of its journey is less sweet. Spoiler alert: it involves clinging to the inner walls (in fear/confusion perhaps, if I were to anthropomorphize the bees . . .) rather than flying—and ends sadly, in death.

The story goes like this: the third test flight of Columbia, launched on March 22, 1982, was the inaugural moment in which bees were pitched beyond the border of our planetary homeland and into space. The journey lasted eight days with an orbit altitude of one hundred and forty-seven nautical miles (sorry metric-oriented space fans, that's the unit of measure nasa.gov provides). While the story of bees in space starts with failure, eventually the studies end up with bees successful in progressing and learning, resilient little buzzers they are!

The next time around, instead of only bringing fourteen bees, Discovery shuttled thirty-four hundred bees into space, more than two hundred and forty times as many! Did all of them die? No, not this time. Thank goodness. Only one hundred and fifty of them passed away during the tough journey. That's only a fraction of the thousands brought by Discovery.

In terms of study objectives, the bees fared a bit better flying-wise, but built strange structures, angled in unusual ways. For example, one of the combs displayed a strange duality of angles, with cells on one side of the comb angled up and the other side angled down. What is up and down in this scenario anyway, since they're off-Earth?

In this case, up refers to the glass/plastic top sheet of the Bee Enclosure and down is towards the floor of the module. Besides this phenomenon of opposing angles on each side, they also created comb pieces showcasing various angles. The results of the experiment suggest the honeybees couldn't tell up from down, or at least encountered some difficulty. It may be safe to say that bees in outer space were pretty turned around, without gravity to orient them. That's one of the lessons, zero-G messes with your head . . . or wings! While Conrad's article discusses in detail how these space bees fared, the message at the end is sobering. The last sentence is a cautionary tale to take care of our own planet . . . probably with Earthside colony collapse and ecological disasters in mind.

Moving to bees' incredible architecture constructions, they have even inspired human's technological prowess into space. Did the engineers of the James Webb telescope "comb" the biodiversity of Earth's fauna to design the telescope? Why, yes, they did!

The James Webb telescope's mirrored surfaces are, in fact, based in part on bee hives. When these mirrors interlock, the hexagonal shapes come together approaching a circle shape without leaving gaps, an ideal structure for an unfolding telescope. This striking visual imagery of Webb-as-honeycomb inspired me to paint a science fictional Queen Bee pollinating a "Webb" honeycomb-like flower, made of hexagonal mirrors. I'm not alone on this pull to draw bees back into the equation, when artistically rendering that mission. Other artists have taken to the mirrors and their buzzing insect counterparts, drawing inventive bees and telescopes, such as "microverse of bees" by Andrés Guerrero and its trippy spiky ball-like hive referencing the Webb and Joanna Barnum's series of watercolor with gold leaf that reference the Webb, including one entitled "Icon: Metaphor" that depicts busy bees pollinating flowers that decorate a "wreath" of the Webb telescope.

Another way in which bees have inspired technology in space is in their industriousness, collective activity, and role-specific uniformity. NASA's cleverly named Astrobee system comprises of three cube-shaped robots that are just those types of workers. Identical except by color and equipped with three payload bays and nine ports for future hardware, two of the robots, Honey and Bumble, launched in April 2019, do routine chores around the ISS: reporting anomalies, shlepping cargo, checking inventory and accumulating cartographic data to test spatial orientation. Mostly they're a testbed for other robots to come. They fly with electric fans and have perching arms that can help their human astronaut co-workers. Their docking station was launched earlier, in November 2018, and installed in the Japanese Experiment Module in February 2019, to be ready for their arrival. Queen, the third member of the group, joined the pair later in July 2019. Queen boasts three perching arms and has taken panoramic photos of the inside of the ISS. Though named Queen, she's not averse to rolling up her sleeves and getting dirty, figuratively-speaking, as she serves as an integral part of the robot cube team. The three free-flying bots work as part of as a collective in the Astrobee system, and thus demonstrate bee-like collaborative labor.

So, bees have staked their claim in space, whether as actual animals pitched into less-than-ideal gravity situations, bee-inspired and -named robots to do pivotal testing and work in the ISS, or as triumphs of architecture manifested in human technological prowess, i.e. the Webb telescope.

Have they staked their claim in science-fictional space? To some degree, yes. I've already mentioned some artwork. Let's talk about fiction.

Humans and Aliens as Bees: Hives and Hive Minds in Outer Space and Underground

Barrington J. Bayley writes of a protagonist that explores a honeycomb and eventually becomes endowed with hive mind perception by way of ingesting honey-cake-like "honey of experience" in "The Bees of Knowledge." Space bees appear in this story (among some SF fiction tropes involving bodily functions and probing), as the story begins in outer space.

Rocked by an explosion in the engine room of their interstellar craft, this catastrophe pitches the protagonist into the strange world of knowledgeable and powerful giant bees, intellectually gifted but possibly bereft of human understanding. Physiologically, they appear like real bees to some extent: striped, fuzzy and golden. Math communication is featured here, though I wonder if maybe the protagonist should have danced, as the giant bees did earlier in the story, "waggling" and "wailing", to communicate.

The hive mind in this story involves not only the consciousness or visions of the giant bees, but also that of the protagonist, as well as other species. Fractured memories come to form in physical manifestations, though it may be a hallucination, catalyzed by the honey consumption as I understand it, though the causation of the series of events could be differently interpreted.

Often, the hive mind is used abstractly to discuss a shared intellect or consciousness, without mention of bees specifically. One famous instance of a hive mind by abstraction rather than accompanied by actual bee-like physiology is the Borg Collective in *Star Trek*. Their aptly named "Hive Mind" or collective consciousness, in which multiple species share knowledge and intelligence as to be almost an individual mind in control.

Another early example in written fiction is the race of Selenites in H.G. Wells, *The First Men in the Moon*. The Selenites are based off insects, such as bees, and operate with mechanical efficiency, also much like an individual mind manipulating all. These are alien examples, but humans can become bee-like, too.

Sci-Fi Humans-Turned-Bees: Physiology

Will humans become honeybees? The space opera film *Jupiter Ascending* says yes, or at least half-bee for select superhumans. Besides enhanced physical traits such as flight, super speed and unique sight bestowed upon Stinger Apini, the half-honeybee character, the film also highlights bee social traits such as loyalty and their architectural competence in constructing hives in the litany of his transformed attributes.

In "An Urge to Create Honey" by Martin Cahill, extraterrestrial hive minds are characterized as a "library of minds, its many souls all working in harmony" that the second-person POV once-human protagonist experiences after new physiological developments (vocal cords, hairs) that allows them to process data, hum and buzz and fit into the alien hive that has taken them in. Honey, here, changes people into bee aliens, and bestows upon them the impulse to share one of the goals of the hive: to be one of the honey producers as well.

Aliens as Bees: Metaphorical Pollination and Bee Color Patterning

In the span of one Earth rotation, i.e. a day, one honeybee can pollinate five thousand flowers and a colony can pollinate up to three hundred million flowers. That's quite a number! Aliens are also bees, in a metaphorical sense in Isaac Asimov's "Does a Bee Care?" in that they pollinate. Pollination here is used more broadly, as a kind of inadvertent seeding. An ovum left on Earth by aliens takes the shape of a human, named Kane. Kane unwittingly influences the eventual humans without them discovering his provenance. Here Kane eventually does the "pollinating," i.e. incidentally driving space travel progress and bringing his own alien self back to his homeland somewhere in space. Yes, aliens are bees here, non-human creatures, but the main characteristic of bees brought into the limelight is their ability to pollinate without realizing, unintentionally galvanizing ecological and technological impact.

In a popular cinematic franchise, there's smart-aleck Bumblebee from Transformers, both alien and mechanical at once and can transform into various kinds of cars and cooperate with other Autobots. The bee reference is mostly likely more due to Bumblebee's color patterning and smaller size than anything else, though one could argue his capability, reliability, and tenacity are common traits of bees.

Beyond Written Fiction

Space bees and hive minds appear in all kinds of media that use science fiction narratives. In *Rick and Morty*, the character, Unity, is a hive mind that can seize control of other species' minds and can easily use the species members as literal talking heads, switching mouths to finish each other's sentences. Here, hive minds can develop deep, romantic connections with humans, as the Unity professes love to Rick.

In addition to animated TV shows, hive minds have made their way into both video and board games. Rachni Queens in the RPG, *Mass Effect 3*, set in the Milky Way galaxy in 2186, run their species through hive minds, guiding with their matriarchal prowess in the face of less hospitable planetary environments. Burrowed underground in nests, they lay eggs and mesmerize with telepathic melodies (and captivating glowing eyes).

Space bees called Mellifera (originating from a futuristic human-less Earth) live in hives and labor endlessly, traveling into space, until they are too exhausted to do more than hibernate in the board game *Apiary*.

In this game, worker bees in each player's faction buzz around busily in space, collecting fiber, pollen, and water to produce wax and honey. They create dances to communicate with one another. They hibernate and shed husks. Collaboratively, they share a QueenShip and explore the galaxy, making positive changes to each planet they visit and inhabit. They're truly Solarpunk . . . or maybe Space-Flowerpunk, seeding life in barren planets, imbuing lushness to otherwise fallow rocks. Terraforming, cute and punky, these bees are sure to please!

The gameplay involves resource collection, tile-laying and worker placement. The tiles are hexagon-shaped, one of the configurations of tile-laying that allows for all edges to touch without spaces, and as a bonus, are appropriately hive-cell-oriented in construction. The game's as adorable and charismatic as their species-member counterparts! Create wondrous civilizational art through carvings! Learn some new dances!

If you're looking to fight space bees from the comfort of your PC/ Console, ahem I mean spacecraft, you might try your hand at the old-school type of shoot 'em up game, *Space Bees* 太空蜜蜂 or the old video game *Captain Comic* to recover treasures taken from the planet

Omsoc and relocated to the remote planet Tambi, where in the course your journey, you will encounter killer bees to defeat.

If you want to be a bee, maybe play as humanoid bee-like Abeil in *Dungeons and Dragons*, though granted, this is more leaning toward fantasy than bees in space, but possibly, import the race into your home-brew space opera RPG!

The manifestations of science fictional bees in various forms of media attest to the appeal of bees and their collective *distinctive* attributes (that paradoxically make them somewhat *indistinct* individually, at least when it comes to hive minds) and will continue to buzz about in space, in our texts, films and games, doing dances in our cultural consciousness.

ABOUT THE AUTHOR

D.A. Xiaolin Spires steps into portals and reappears in sites such as Hawai'i, NY, various parts of Asia and elsewhere, with her keyboard appendage attached. Her work appears in publications such as *Clarkesworld, Analog, Nature, Terraform, Fireside, Star*Line, Liquid Imagination,* and anthologies such as *Make Shift, Ride the Star Wind, Sharp and Sugar Tooth, Deep Signal,* and *Battling in All Her Finery.* Select stories can be read in German, Spanish, Vietnamese, Estonian, French and Japanese translation.

Hoodoo And Physics:
A Conversation with Andrea Hairston

ARLEY SORG

Andrea Hairston was born in Pittsburgh PA and lived there until she
attended Smith College at the age of eighteen. At Smith she studied
physics and math before earning her BA in Theatre. She earned an MA
in Creative Writing at Brown—the program now gives an MFA—with
a focus on playwriting; but she also studied screenwriting and film.
Hairston studied German for three years and then began going to
Germany. She went to the Goethe-Institut in Prien (a small town in
Bavaria) and started spending summers in Munich and its environs. "In

1995 I was a Guest Professor at the Universität Hamburg and I taught a course on Black Women Playwrights and worked with someone who was directing *Faust*."

Andrea Hairston's debut novel *Mindscape* was published by Aqueduct Press in 2006. It was nominated for an Otherwise Award, was a Philip K. Dick Award finalist, and won a Carl Brandon Parallax Award. *Redwood and Wildfire* (Aqueduct 2011; re-released by Tordotcom Publishing in 2022) landed on the Locus Recommended Reading list and won both the Otherwise and Carl Brandon Awards. *Will Do Magic For Small Change* (Aqueduct 2016; Tordotcom 2022) was a finalist for Mythopoeic, Lambda, and Otherwise Awards; it was also a Massachusetts Must Read, and a New York Times Editor's pick. Tordotcom published *Master of Poisons* in 2020 to critical acclaim and starred reviews, and the novel landed on the *Kirkus* Best Books of 2020 list.

Besides being a respected fiction writer, Hairston is also a playwright, with work produced at Yale Rep, Rites and Reason, the Kennedy Center, StageWest, and on Public Radio and Television. Aqueduct published a collection of "Two Plays, a Speech, and Eight Essays" called *Lonely Stardust* in 2014. Hairston has received grants from the National Endowment for the Arts, the Rockefeller Foundation, the Ford Foundation, and the Massachusetts Cultural Council. She won a Distinguished Scholarship Award from the International Association for the Fantastic in the Arts in 2011, and she is the Louise Wolff Kahn 1931 Professor Emerita of Theatre and Africana Studies at Smith College and the Artistic Director of Chrysalis Theatre.

Andrea Hairston's latest novel, *Archangels of Funk*, is due from Tordotcom Publishing this month.

Have you gone full-time writer, or do you still have a day job? Have you had other cool, interesting, boring, or surprising jobs?

I am just a full-time writer now!

I was a math textbook editor at Houghton Mifflin after I graduated from Smith. I worked there for ten months until I headed off to graduate study at Brown. I was the first Black person in the math division. An alien experience. No one really talked to me until I was about to leave. Although someone did ask if I could lose a razor blade in my afro. Pam Grier put the fear of death in folks! This was the mid-seventies and Houghton Mifflin paid the women editors less than the men. However, whenever they wanted quality/overtime work for an impending deadline, they asked the women editors to come in on the weekends. They also told a bunch of mathematicians not to talk about our salaries with each other. So of course, I/we wanted to know what they were keeping from us. The women editors pressed a class action suit. I got a settlement after I finished graduate school. I used it to buy a balaphone—a West African xylophone.

I have done theatre with a range of folks, helping them create plays based on their life stories, their struggles, triumphs, heartbreaks, and joys: I've worked with recovering addicts, pregnant and parenting teens, at-risk youth, overworked social workers, and asylum seekers in Germany.

Boredom isn't really one of my modes.

The summer before my junior or senior year in college, I supervised a group of at-risk youth who were doing community clean-up, clearing brush, and spearing garbage in Springfield, MA. Funky work, but we had an amazing time. They were writing poems and monologues by the end of the summer and doing spoken word performances.

I've done theatre all over. Putting up productions, there were always many back-breaking, dirty, repetitive tasks. Hanging blacks (dark curtains) for instance, to transform a bright all-purpose room with windows and white walls into a black box theatre. I had to climb up a 25-foot-tall ladder with yards and yards of thick, dusty velour! Weighty chains at the bottom keep the fabric taut and immobile and ropes at the top are used to tie them in place. I had to tie *really* good knots. For a fifty by fifty room that had to be blacked out, that was a lot of up and down. Someone footed the ladder, but had trouble with heights, so it was me going up to the top.

In addition to tech, in rehearsal, directors have to listen to the same lines over and over! And then there is grant writing to secure the funds to climb the ladders and hang the black velour so the performers can dazzle the audience. But the show must go on!

You decided to write science fiction when you were a guest profes-
sor at the University of Hamburg. Archangels of Funk is your fifth
novel. What are the most important things you've learned about
writing and publishing across the course of five novels?

Keep on keeping on! Rewrite till you get it right. Stick to your vision and find the best way to express yourself.

Has your writing changed in important ways since Mindscape, or since your more recent novel, Master of Poisons? And what are the reasons for those changes?

Every book I write is an adventure. I learn so much about myself and the world. I am changed as a writer and as a person. How I write each novel depends on the story I have to tell and the state of the world and me in the world. In *Mindscape* I was struggling with the Poet, Playwright, and Screenwriter, trying to become a Novelist. Writing *Archangels of Funk*, I wasn't struggling with that. All my writer selves were happy. I need the Poet, Playwright, Screenwriter, and Novelist to tell the story that's breaking my mind open.

Who do you see as your literary influences, and do you feel like these influences (or other influences) show up in Archangels of Funk in important ways?

I am influenced by everyone and everything I encounter. My writing is an embodiment of my engagement with the world—conscious or unconscious. I rely on a multitude of insights from my human and nonhuman world community—and that's across time and space. I have an extended mind—and there's a book with that title that I love. *The Extended Mind* by Annie Murphy Paul. I loved this book because it matched what I was thinking, but also because it took me to new and startling places as well. Playwrights like Pearl Cleage extend my mind with their plays. *Flyin' West* is one of Pearl's plays that I love. In *Archangels of Funk*, a character has a role in that play. Pearl has people coming up with the world they want in the face of ridiculous odds and worse circumstances! Nalo Hopkinson, Sheree Renée Thomas, Pan Morigan, Nisi Shawl, and Octavia Butler do that in their fiction. And so do Daniel José Older, Annalee Newitz, Tananarive Due, and Martha Wells. These writers, making that way out of no way, inspire me!

I told myself I couldn't read Wells' *Murderbot Diaries* until after finishing *Archangels*. I was dying to read them, so this was a great incentive. When I sent the manuscript to my editor, I got to binge on *Murderbot*. I didn't have to wait for the next volume to come out. A serious reward!

Of course, I am also influenced by the actions, events, proclamations, books, tweets, and films that bother me, work my nerves, make me want to scream.

What was the initial inspiration for Archangels of Funk, and what were some of the most significant changes from concept and first draft to final product?

I was at a gathering of Afrofuturists at Princeton University: Black to the Future, and I imagined a Seventh Generations Algorithm and a tech nerd living in a dumb house and traveling salespeople trying to sell her obsolete tech that she had helped design. I wrote two short stories using these ideas. I turned the short stories into a play—that translation was a great challenge for building the story and developing the characters. I did a staged reading of the play. Actors, wow, they breathe life into your story! All the wonderful stuff I thought of for the play I had to translate back to fiction for the novel. Translating and transforming the story for different modalities is a wonderful, rich process!

What were the biggest challenges in writing this book, and how did you deal with those challenges?

Writing a Festival, trying to bring a carnival to life in prose!

The starred Library Journal review for Archangels praises your prose and specifically, its musicality. In terms of craft, what is the key to writing great prose?

I don't know if there's a key. For me it's loving words and their expressive capacities. I am a voracious word hound. I read fiction and nonfiction. I savor everyday speech and elegant prose, spoken word poetry and ancient plays. I love films and radio/podcast shows. I have studied several languages and I am fluent in German. Learning a language is a portal to another world. I love to explore a character's idiom, how a particular culture or time favors certain metaphors. Language is how we experience, define, and recreate the world, the universe. Language is the poetic embodiment of all the speakers who invented it and the people using it right now.

Master of Poisons received heaps of praise, such as Publishers Weekly lauding its "stirring prose" and calling it "an urgent, gorgeous work." For folks who loved Master of Poisons, are there important similarities and differences between that book and Archangels of Funk?

Each of my novels has a specific voice, a particular character. But that said, I am an Afrofuturist in league with Indigenous-Futurists. I always have African and Indigenous ancestors talking to the future. I always call on hoodoo and physics to create my story universe. Afrofuturism is at the core of *Archangels of Funk*. Animal-people POV characters have been coming to me since *Master of Poisons* and other non-human POV characters since *Will Do Magic For Small Change*. So all of that figures into *Archangels of Funk*. And to quote Annalee Newitz—*Archangels* is about a future of ambient queerness and eco-anarchy!

What else are you working on, what do you have out or coming up that you'd like Clarkesworld readers to know about?

I have written about two thirds of my next novel: *The Redemption Center is Closed on Sunday*, a murder mystery. One of the detective types is a cleaning lady and another is a search-and-rescue carnival dog. And of course, time and space are warped. Hoodoo and physics. I am also taking notes for another book in the *Archangels of Funk* world. Can't get enough of that funky stuff!

ABOUT THE AUTHOR

Arley Sorg is an associate agent at kt literary. He is a two-time World Fantasy Award Finalist and a two-time Locus Award Finalist for his work as co-Editor-in-Chief at *Fantasy Magazine*. Arley is also a SFWA Solstice Award Recipient, a Space Cowboy Award Recipient, and a finalist for two Ignyte Awards. Arley is senior editor at *Locus*, associate editor at both *Lightspeed* & *Nightmare*, a columnist for *The Magazine of Fantasy and Science Fiction* and an interviewer for *Clarkesworld*. He is a guest critiquer for the 2023 Odyssey Workshop, and is the week five instructor for the 2023 6-week Clarion West Workshop, among other teaching and speaking engagements.

Science Fiction
As Science Communication:
A Conversation with Andrea Kriz

ARLEY SORG

Andrea Kriz was born in Chicago and grew up in Michigan. Her parents as well as three of her grandparents all earned PhDs: "Growing up, I thought that getting a PhD and dedicating your life to research was normal . . . " Kriz earned her B.S. in Biology at MIT and a PhD in Biological and Biomedical Sciences at Harvard. Her studies included a concentration in linguistics at MIT as part of the Humanities, Arts, and Social Sciences requirement.

Kriz has garnered a number of accolades beyond genre circles. In 2015 she received the MIT undergraduate Ilona Karmel Prize (now called the King Prize) for Writing Science Fiction. She also received the AMITA (Association of MIT Alumnae) 2015 Senior Academic Award. As a PhD student she landed fellowships from various organizations, such as the National Science Foundation (NSF) and National Institutes of Health (NIH); then later, the Jane Coffin Childs fellowship, as a postdoctoral researcher.

Andrea Kriz hit the SFF short fiction scene with "Chrysalis" as her first publication, which came out at *Nature* in February of 2016. She continued to publish steadily, often with several stories appearing in a year across a range of venues. Examples include more appearances in *Nature*; "Waiting for Superman" in *Daily Science Fiction* in 2017; "Pearleater's Promise" in *Cossmass Infinities* in 2020; and her first of several appearances in *Clarkesworld*, "Communist Computer Rap God" in 2021. She has also had fiction appear at *Lightspeed*, *Asimov's*, *Diabolical Plots*, *Fireside*, and more. Her French resistance alternate history story, "The Leviathan and the Fury" (originally published in *Asimov's*) was translated into French and published in *Galaxies SF* in January 2023. "I had a wonderful experience working with a translator, Fred Gevart, who suggested edits to make the symbolism work better for French readers. They also ended up making the story stronger overall. I ended up incorporating these into the English version of the story which will be published in my collection."

Besides her strong track record in genre fiction, Kriz has an impressive set of biological research publications. "Fun fact, I've been published in the journal *Nature* both as an author on a scientific article as well as a science fiction author." She currently does postdoctoral research in brain genetics at Harvard Medical School.

Debut short story collection *Learning to Hate Yourself as a Self-Defense Mechanism* is due from Interstellar Flight Press this month.

What were the books or stories that were important to you when you were younger, and do you see them as literary influences, or are your influences very different?

Animorphs is the first science fiction series I remember really getting into, and also the first one I remember that really inspired me to speculate. (What would it be like to be controlled for decades by a Yeerk? Or to be permanently morphed into a hawk?) I read *2666* by Roberto Bolaño in high school (probably too young), and it completely changed my perception of what a novel can be. It was the first book I read where basically every facet of character motivation, and even the plot, is left up to reader interpretation. It was a brutal experience. Anime was also a huge influence on me when I was younger (and continues to be!). When I watched *Neon Genesis Evangelion* as a high schooler, I was so fascinated by the psychology of the Angels and how they try to communicate with humans—particularly how they communicate with Rei, who has a cloned human body but an Angel soul. Even after watching *The End of Evangelion,* I had so many questions that I was unable to find satisfying answers for, despite scouring the internet. The only recourse I had was to endlessly speculate. Eventually, when I started writing, I found myself using those same kinds of speculative muscles and striving to create work that would spur the same kinds of emotions in other people.

In the acknowledgements for Learning to Hate Yourself as a Self-Defense Mechanism, one of the people you thank is Shariann Lewitt, "for introducing me to the world of speculative short fiction . . . " What has your writer's journey been like? Were there times when you struggled, and what continues to bring you back?

I started seriously writing near the end of college, but for some reason it never occurred to me to write science fiction or fantasy (despite reading a lot of it). That all changed when I took a Fiction Workshop class with Shariann Lewitt in my senior year. Shariann introduced me to the world of speculative fiction magazines, some of which are sadly not around anymore—shout-outs to *Fantastic Stories of the Imagination, Daily Science Fiction, Lightspeed,* and of course *Clarkesworld*! These were the first venues I read regularly. I was in absolute awe at the sheer creativity and power portrayed in each story in so few words. The last piece fell into place when I was reading an issue of *Nature* and saw that they published science fiction! I vividly remember reading *Bread of Life* by Beth Cato and having my heart torn out by an entire story packed into a single page. Reading short fiction inspired me to write and led to my first publication in *Nature Futures* in 2016 (though I can't condone the exorbitantly high paywalls they now unfortunately put on most of their stories).

Most of my stories were written while I was doing my PhD. In a way my PhD and writing complemented each other, as when my research wasn't going well, I could turn to my writing and vice versa. It was also difficult though, because both academia and writing involve a lot of rejection. Starting in 2016, there were things going on in the world that increasingly impacted my life and prevented me from focusing on writing or doing science. I struggled with that many times. Then, of course, 2020 happened. I had just received (challenging) peer reviews back for my PhD paper when the world shut down. What kept me going was a feeling really aptly summarized by the song "Look at the Sky" by Porter Robinson. So many crazy things are happening in the world that I can't say where I'll be in even ten years. But I'm here now and I can make a promise to myself that I'll be here next year. In that time, I can make something good.

There are a few pieces of media I keep coming back to when the writing journey gets tough. Porter Robinson's album *Nurture* is one of the most accurate portrayals of the creative process I've experienced. It touches on struggles that I think will ring true for a lot of writers: the come-down after initial success, questioning yourself for not being content with success you've already had, feeling like you'll never live up to your initial success, growing as an artist independently of expectations (yours and others', real or perceived), and creating for the sake of creating. Something else I've found more recently is the manga *Look Back* by Tatsuki Fujimoto. The main character, Fujino, gives up on drawing manga after another student at her school draws "better" art than her. The panel where Fujino dances in the rain after learning that her perceived artistic rival was actually inspired by her manga is immensely powerful to me.

For you, what is special about or specific to science fiction?

I'm excited about science fiction as a means of science communication, particularly beyond "cautionary tale" stories. So many people are distrustful of science, especially the biological sciences, and sometimes that can be justified but I think a lot of the time it can be rooted in misunderstanding—not because people don't want to understand science, but because they might not have the right resources accessible to them. Not everyone is going to be able to delve into a scientific paper, but a lot of people love engaging with fiction that speculates on where current research may take us in the future. Narratives about worst-case scenarios, lone geniuses, and mad scientists have their place but I love science fiction that goes beyond that and tries to portray science with all its nuances and ups and downs. A few short story examples I'm a big fan of: "Best-Laid Plans" by David D. Levine and all of Arula Ratnakar's fiction. I also love how fantasy involving magical research and academia can delve into these topics, like *Babel* by R.F. Kuang.

I love encouraging researchers to engage with science fiction, whether that's writing it, reading it, or even talking with fans. Thinking creatively and speculation are often essential for advancing science. However, research can also have long ruts that make it difficult to engage with that creativity—that's why I think stepping out of the lab (at least occasionally!) is essential. I also love to encourage authors to reach out to researchers working in the fields they're interested in writing about, in a respectful way—never underestimate how eager a scientist is to talk about their work!

As a scientist, is scientific plausibility important to your stories? Do you seek it out and expect it in the science fiction you enjoy?

I do have a compulsion to be as scientifically accurate as possible when I write about biology, which has perhaps hindered me from writing a lot of biological science fiction, haha. I don't think a story has to be 100% scientifically accurate to be enjoyable, but one does need to avoid getting the basics wrong. For example, I really enjoyed "The Dragon Project" by Naomi Kritzer even without in-depth biological explanations of how all the dragons were being created. However, if a story pivots on bioengineering and a character inaccurately explains what DNA is, for example, then that will take me out of it.

Even before your first published story you won a prize for writing science fiction back in 2015. Looking at your body of work, including the collection at hand, are there themes, motifs, or ideas that you tend to come back to? Or are the concerns of each story very different from the next?

I think "unhealthy coping mechanisms" is a theme that runs through many of my stories (especially those featured in my collection—see the title). "The Ones Who Got Away from Time and Loss" features a series of researchers who travel back in time to steal their peers' work rather than face a scientific world where they aren't the first to make a discovery. In "Rebuttal to Reviewers' comments..." a scientist addresses negative peer reviews about her human-to-dragon transmutation study in a dramatically fiery way. Most of these stories were written when I was a PhD student, when I was becoming increasingly immersed in the academic world. I reflected a lot on what it means to be successful scientifically, and how the current system doesn't always reward or even encourage sharing knowledge and doing good science. Despite that, there is still amazing science being done and people who persevere in trying to make the system better.

Many of my stories also feature creatives trying to cope in a perpetually online world that sees their art as "content" to be "consumed." In "Communist Computer Rap God," a YouTuber ends up becoming the scapegoat for the behavior of the titular AI he created (who also ends up becoming a more popular YouTuber than him). In "There Are No Hot Topics on Whukai," a marginalized gamer is hired to help a fanfic author's work appear more "authentic" to the online community. I think a lot of creatives are conditioned to put their personal lives online in the hopes of "going viral," seeing this as the only way to "make it"—but going viral can often have extremely negative consequences. I know this hope of going viral versus its potential devastating consequences is something I'm still grappling with personally.

Learning to Hate Yourself as a Self-Defense Mechanism *includes twelve stories—eleven reprints and one original. What was the process or organizational principle behind selecting stories and the order in which they appear in the book?*

Most of the stories in the first part of the collection portray coping in an extremely negative way. In the titular story, which kicks off the collection, You are a game creator grappling with an accusation of racism from someone You saw as a very close friend, someone who turns out to have incorporated private moments of Your relationship into their own (award-winning) games. The title is self-explanatory. Self-hate appears in a lot of the subsequent stories as well.

I see the last three stories of the collection, however, as turning the page. "Resistance in a Drop of DNA," "The Last Caricature of Jean Moulin," and "The Leviathan and the Fury" are all alternative history stories about the French Resistance during World War II, one of the darkest periods of history. The characters in these three stories all go through similar traumatic losses, but finally we see them acknowledging their grief and flaws—and perhaps moving on?

In a way, it's easy to end a story depressingly, when a character is at their lowest point completely due to their own doing. These days, however, I find myself wondering, what comes after? In real life, people don't magically disappear after ruining their lives. I find myself trying more and more to write about what comes next.

What can you tell us about the original story, "And That's Why I Gave Up on Magic," without spoiling the read too much?

The story was inspired by the song "That's Why I Gave Up on Music" by Yorushika and the anime *Eighty-Six*. The cover art of my collection was also inspired by the original story! Shout-outs to the cover artist, Dante Luiz, who is an amazing artist and person to work with! And special thanks to the editors and proofreaders at Interstellar Flight Press who helped make this story the best it can be :)

Are there one or two stories here which you are particularly excited for new readers to discover, and why?

I'm excited for readers to discover "And That's Why I Gave Up on Magic," as it's the first time this story will be shared with the world. I'd also love to recommend "Rebuttal to Reviewers' Comments . . . " to researchers or anyone curious about what the peer review process is like for science (with the follow-up questions of, how did this go right and where did this go wrong?)

Which stories in the collection were most challenging to write? What made them challenging, and how did you face those challenges?

In a way "The Leviathan and the Fury" is kind of a thesis of all the historical research I did during 2020-2021, thanks to having a lot of unexpected free time at home and to the Harvard libraries making many of their books available to checkout online. The story centers around what would've happened if the French Resistance leader, Jean Moulin, had survived the war, told from the point of view from someone personally mourning him. There are probably hundreds of alternative timelines integrated into the story, so I had to cut a lot of details out. I coped with that by telling myself that one day I could write a longer story or a book elaborating on them more in-depth, haha.

There are a number of authors who are known specifically for their short fiction, and some who have little interest in novels. Are you working on novel-length projects as well? Or do you see yourself primarily as a short fiction author?

Yes! I recently finished polishing a novel and started seeking representation for it. The novel is about a university student who manifests DNA-manipulating magic and must make a choice: "volunteer" to fight in a never-ending war, piloting a mecha with her new powers, or wear a magic-repressor seal marking her as a coward. She chooses to wear the seal and continue her research, hoping to discover a way to end the war, but the military police coerces her to spy on her fellow students. Eventually she teams up with her research advisor, a biology professor, melding magic and science to tear down the racist system that entrapped them both. I put my love of the biological sciences into this novel and really hope I can share that with readers one day.

What else are you working on, what do you have out or coming up that Clarkesworld readers should know about?

I had the chance last year (2023) to participate in the Dartmouth Speculative Fiction Project, a collaboration between authors and Dartmouth faculty to create short stories exploring the future of humanity. This was an amazing opportunity which tapped into a lot of hopes I personally have for speculative fiction and how it can serve as a means of science communication to the public. I really hope that more universities across the world become inspired to follow in Dartmouth's footsteps and connect their faculty with authors and vice versa!

I have a new story coming out in *Lightspeed Magazine* in June, "Udo Gehler and the Virgin Bitch of the Resistance," which I would love to share with readers. It's a mecha story set in a fractured America, where one side has industrialized an Evangelion-like mecha system, relying on forced birth.

ABOUT THE AUTHOR

Arley Sorg is an associate agent at kt literary. He is a two-time World Fantasy Award Finalist and a two-time Locus Award Finalist for his work as co-Editor-in-Chief at *Fantasy Magazine*. Arley is also a SFWA Solstice Award Recipient, a Space Cowboy Award Recipient, and a finalist for two Ignyte Awards. Arley is senior editor at *Locus*, associate editor at both *Lightspeed* & *Nightmare*, a columnist for *The Magazine of Fantasy and Science Fiction* and an interviewer for *Clarkesworld*. He is a guest critiquer for the 2023 Odyssey Workshop, and is the week five instructor for the 2023 6-week Clarion West Workshop, among other teaching and speaking engagements.

Editor's Desk: Fruit of the Tree
NEIL CLARKE

Last month, I had to write two editorials that painted different visions of the future: one darker and another representing whatever we're in now. I'd never thought I'd say this, but I'm happy to be writing an entirely new one this month. While we escaped having to run the bleaker version of events, the reprieve remains temporary. The delays, however, mean something is working to our advantage. At worst, we've bought time and that's being well-spent on things that may minimize the effect of what I still can't talk about.

Instead, this month I'm going to talk about one of the other problems we have. It's hardly a surprise when I talk about generative "AI" these days. It remains an ongoing problem for us with regards to submissions, but in talking with other genre editors, it doesn't seem to have spread to other markets as quickly as it could have. The most likely reason for this is that the community responsible for much of these submissions remains largely unaware of them. Those of us hit the hardest had the misfortune of being the few genre magazines on a small number of lists not typically used by science fiction writers or publishers. When I worked in technology, we joked about "security through obscurity." It can work for a time, but shouldn't be relied upon. The tide could turn at any time.

Unfortunately, this isn't a problem that will just go away. Even if the courts or our governments decide that the development of these technologies was done in violation of the copyrights of millions—something many of us believe—it doesn't prevent the creation of so-called "ethically-trained" models that utilize licensed data. (We'll sidestep the whole issue of the massive data grab that is happening as part of usage agreements in major online community applications. Legal, perhaps. Ethical?) Some form of this technology will continue to be developed and power the spam of tomorrow.

Where does that leave us?

If we look at the problem, what we're facing isn't really new. I've been calling these submissions "spam" and that's very much part of that family. We've been dealing with email and comment spam for a long time. Submission spam is just the new hustle. We manage the other spam with filtering tools. If you were an active email user in the late nineties or early aughts, you might even remember some outcry about the ethics of introducing spam filters or statements about how they would impact "free speech." Ultimately, these tools became normalized due to their benefits outweighing any perceived negatives.

Even decades after spam filters were first created, they still make mistakes. We're supposed to browse our spam folders periodically as a check against the automation, but not everyone does that. The stakes are different for an individual vs a university admissions office or most businesses. Many small magazines still accept submissions via email and have a responsibility to check those folders periodically to make sure an author's email hasn't been inappropriately categorized.

Generative "AI" spam is going to be no different. Editors are going to have to accept flawed processes that make it possible for them to do their jobs and be responsible for reviewing what gets marked as such. At *Clarkesworld*, we're already doing this, but at a very primitive level. Submissions are split into two queues—regular and suspicious—and reviewed by humans. Suspicious submissions are reviewed less frequently, so the worst that happens to a miscategorized story is that it takes a bit longer. If something is generated, however, the person is banned. If we aren't sure, they get flagged for review on future submissions and treated like anyone else. If the filter got it wrong, I move it to the regular queue and see what we can learn from the experience to decrease the rate of false positives.

It's worked well so far. We've seen more than a few surges since implementing the system and our two-queue model has worked like a pressure valve. The false positive rate is still higher than I like, but it's correct often enough to be beneficial. All this has been done without the benefit of the various AI detection tools that are on the market. I won't explain what we have been doing to figure out what is "suspicious" but I will say that it hasn't just caught "AI" spam, but also plagiarism and some other forms of fraud as well.

The decision not to use commercial detection tools was easy. Despite the marketing claims, the majority of the detectors we tested were extremely unreliable. False positives and false negatives were rampant and, as has been since confirmed by a university study, many of these products suffered from a tendency to misidentify works from non-native English language writers as AI generated. Given our interest in recruiting authors from all over the world, this was a significant strike against adoption. If that wasn't enough, we discovered that several of these tools were collecting submitted works to use as training data or worse.

The publicity around what happened to us put us on the radar of a lot of people who are interested in tackling this problem. Over the last year, I've spoken with dozens of professionals in different fields, some of which offered advice (much of which we've used) and others who were curious about what it would take to make an "acceptable" detector. The big things on my wish list were:

- Does not use or license works submitted for analysis for training purposes without explicit permission.
- Company is respectful of the rights of creatives in all of their products.
- Accuracy, even with non-native English writers.
- Has an API capable of supporting DOCX and RTF files.
- Affordable for a short fiction publication.
- Does not sell a product that prevents generated text from being detected.

I've run into companies that have violated one or more of each of those items, so I haven't been particularly optimistic about it happening. Much to my surprise, however, there are now a couple (one is still being developed, but I've seen it) of products that appear to have checked all the boxes and need to be looked at more closely.

There is a catch, though. The best quality detection requires the developer to use the output of unethically trained systems against it. Their programs consume generated works to find the patterns they can be identified with. It is, in a sense, the grandchild product of stolen data that has been turned against its parent. Even though it helps prevent people from fraudulently passing off generated works as their own, it does pass profit to the people who created the detector. They may have the best of intentions, but does it still cross a line?

While my system has made the task more manageable, it's difficult to replicate and can still be overwhelmed by a sufficient spike in spam. Adding a detector (that meets my specifications) would significantly decrease the false positive rate, improve response times, and allow us to withstand a significant increase in volume. Furthermore, it would be replicable in a way that would help other editors maintain the open submissions practices that have made the short fiction community what it is today.

Open submissions level the playing field, creating opportunities for all authors regardless of how well-known they are to the staff. Should this path to publication close, it would disproportionately impact new authors and those from communities that are not typically represented in the slush piles or pages of most magazines. The loss would ripple outwards from there as short fiction feeds TV, film, novels, and so much more of the field.

Detectors offer one possible path to ensuring that door remains open, but do the benefits outweigh the perceived negatives? Perhaps. Perhaps not. All that is clear is that the need to quickly identify generated text is only going to increase, not just in submissions or email, but across the board. The volume is simply too high and the emotional toll of being suspicious all the time has its downsides too. Something has to change, preferably before things start to break.

I don't have the answers, but I am thinking about it and now, maybe you will too.

ABOUT THE AUTHOR

Neil Clarke is the editor of *Clarkesworld Magazine, Forever Magazine,* and several anthologies, including the Best Science Fiction of the Year series. He is a twelve-time finalist and two-time winner of the Hugo Award for Best Editor (Short Form). He has also won the Chesley Award for Best Art Director four times and received the Kate Wilhelm Solstice Award from SFWA in 2019. His next anthology, *Best Science Fiction of the Year: Volume 8,* will be published later this year by Night Shade Books. He currently lives in NJ with his wife and two sons.

Strider

COVER ART BY ILYA NAZAROV

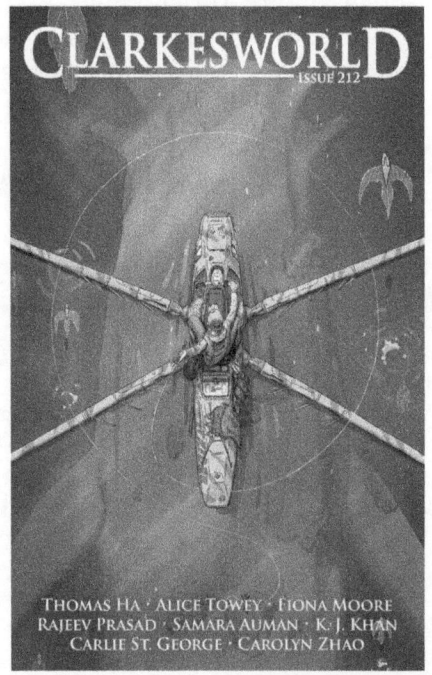

ABOUT THE ARTIST

Ilya Nazarov is a lead concept artist with over nineteen years of industry experience on multiple "Game of The Year" award-winning titles. Some of the games he has worked on include *Starfield, Fallout 76, Fallout 4, Shadow of Mordor, Metroid Prime 2* and *3* and others. Ilya specializes in worldbuilding, storytelling, and design, and has a strong background in 3D art, architecture, and fine art.